ALONG CAME MILLIE

A SPUNKY SENIORS MURDER MYSTERY

JOSHUA BERKOV

Copyright © 2024 by Joshua Berkov

All rights reserved.

No part of this book may be reproduced in any form or by any electronic or mechanical means, including information storage and retrieval systems, without written permission from the author, except for the use of brief quotations in a book review.

Cover designed by Getcovers

❀ Created with Vellum

CONTENTS

Chapter 1	1
Chapter 2	11
Chapter 3	21
Chapter 4	31
Chapter 5	41
Chapter 6	52
Chapter 7	62
Chapter 8	72
Chapter 9	82
Chapter 10	92
Chapter 11	102
Chapter 12	113
Chapter 13	124
Chapter 14	134
Chapter 15	145
Chapter 16	156
Chapter 17	165
Chapter 18	175
Chapter 19	186
Chapter 20	196
Chapter 21	207
Chapter 22	219
Chapter 23	230
Chapter 24	240
Chapter 25	250
Chapter 26	261
Message from the Author	275
Also by Joshua Berkov	277
Acknowledgments	279
About the Author	281

1

I was only supposed to stay a week. One week. That's what my daughter said six months ago, and yet I was still here. You see, six months and one week ago, my house caught fire and burned to the ground. No one was hurt. They blamed it on faulty wiring when all was said and done, which I chose not to contest because what else could I say? I certainly wasn't about to tell my insurance company that I'd hired a non-licensed electrician to add a couple of extra outlets in the basement to support my herbal supplement side hustle. That wouldn't have gone well.

So, my daughter and her husband took me in after the fire since I had nowhere else to go. That was six months and one week ago. Six months and zero weeks ago, my daughter moved me into an already-furnished one-bedroom apartment in a retirement community. I use the term "one-bedroom" loosely here. She said it would be for only a week until she and her husband could rent and furnish an apartment that was *not* in a retirement community for me to live in while my house was being rebuilt. They both knew I despised retirement communities. I asked them why I couldn't continue to stay at their house as I had been doing over the previous week.

"We love you, Mom," my daughter had said. "But we really need our space, and your talents at rearranging furniture, throwing out perfectly good food, setting the thermostat to an optimal temperature for people in their twilight years, turning the volume up on the TV so you can hear it in every room, and telling scary stories that you believe little children will find humorous would be put to better use elsewhere."

I couldn't help the fact that I have a larger-than-life personality, and I certainly wasn't about to change who I was for them. I've always said that you either accept me as I am or you can take your attitude and shove it up where the sun doesn't shine. Well, the problem with this attitude is that it only works when you have the upper hand. Six months ago, I didn't have the upper hand, and I was forced out of my daughter's home and into a blasted retirement community against my will. My daughter and son-in-law had the money and the means to make this happen, so that's exactly what they did.

Oh sure, they tried to convince me that it was just a temporary move while they located a suitable abode for me elsewhere, but I was pretty sure my fate was sealed. You're probably wondering why I didn't take the temporary dwelling money my insurance company owed me per my policy and find a place on my own. Well, you can blame the Raleigh real-estate market for that one. Apartment rents had skyrocketed well beyond what my policy would have paid me, so I was literally dependent on my daughter and son-in-law for help. Plus, I still had a mortgage to pay as well. So, the whole "not having the upper hand" thing really hurt me.

In any event, six months ago on a clear fall day, we drove to a neighboring town where my current abode is located. Springtime Pastures, the name of said abode, billed itself as an active senior community where people of a certain age can live their lives to the fullest. When we first entered the community, I had to admit I was impressed by the charming little bungalows and villas, the well-manicured lawns, and the happy faces plastered all over the residents we passed by as we drove on. I thought perhaps this wasn't going to be so bad after all.

But we kept on driving, my daughter behind the wheel of my car, a twelve-year-old Toyota Camry, and my son-in-law right behind us in his fancy Jaguar. And as we kept on driving, the ambience of the community deteriorated until we finally ended up in front of a building that, I kid you not, looked like a prison. I knew it wasn't a prison, of course, since I was assured that I'd be allowed to keep my own car on the premises and that I'd be able to come and go as I pleased. But the imposing red-brick structure was a far cry from the impeccably kept and obviously newer parts of the community.

I remember turning to my daughter and asking her why she and her husband couldn't have rented me one of those cute houses we had driven by earlier. She tried to convince me that they were all currently occupied and that, since they didn't come furnished, there was really no point in even trying. I didn't buy it. I knew I was being dumped in the cheapest housing Springtime Pastures had to offer, and I made sure my daughter knew that I knew. She pretended to ignore me, launching into a speech about all the wonderful activities I'd have at my disposal here. You know, for a brief moment, I actually considered refusing to get out of the car. But I was afraid they'd send some goons in white shirts armed with tranquilizer darts to subdue me into submission.

As we pulled into a parking spot with a sign in front of it that said "resident," a harried woman came barreling out of the front entrance, clipboard in hand. A skirted white nursing uniform accentuated her voluptuous hips, and her eyes possessed a somewhat vacant expression. She was unusually tall, even from my vantage point still sitting in the front passenger seat of my car, and she wore her blond hair in a short flip bob style that was a little lopsided. *Well, must be part of her charm*, I thought.

"Hi-dee ho!" the woman had said as I apprehensively stepped out of the car. "My name is Julie von Haffen. I'm one of the activities directors here at Springtime Pastures, and specifically, I oversee what we affectionately refer to as the B-Block building where you'll be residing."

Maybe I was wrong, I thought. *Maybe this really is a prison.*

"And you must be my new best friend, Millicent Holt," she continued. "Am I right?"

"Well, that depends, dear," I responded. "You're partially right. I go by 'Millie,' and I already have the two best friends a woman could ever want. Their names are Mary and Jane. So, if you're familiar with them, then perhaps we'll get along. If not, I'm afraid we'll just have to remain acquaintances."

She gave my daughter such a look! Like, *Are you sure you don't want to check out some of the other retirement communities in the area for your mother to stay in?* But my daughter stared right back at her, as if reading her mind, and nodded her head emphatically that this was the place for me. Knowing my daughter as well as I thought I did, I was pretty sure she had put down a nonrefundable deposit to secure the cell they were going to put me in. And I'm betting she did it before the last embers of the fire that consumed my house were put out. So, whether Julie von Haffen liked it or not, I was moving in.

Fortunately, I had very few possessions left to my name, so the actual moving part didn't take long. Two trips back and forth to the car pretty much did the trick, and before I knew it, my daughter and son-in-law sped out of the parking lot so fast they nearly knocked over an elderly woman who was shuffling along on her walker and seemed to be zigzagging around the lot. I wasn't sure if she was doing so intentionally, though. I mean, any number of conditions could have contributed to her lack of direction. A stroke. An inner-ear infection. Ingesting a bit too much of the bourbon she illicitly kept in her room. The possibilities were endless.

I went back up to my new abode shortly thereafter and began the arduous task of unpacking what little I had. Some clothes and shoes I had bought to replace what I had lost in the fire. My medications. A couple of framed pictures I had nicked from my daughter's house without her knowledge. Some snacks I had pilfered from her pantry to tide me over until I could get to the grocery store. Speaking of which, my daughter had promised me I'd have a full kitchen here. I was dismayed to discover all I had was a sink, a refrigerator, and a microwave. I had asked if, perhaps, there was a communal kitchen somewhere in the building, but there wasn't. I'd had to give up my edible herbal supplement business as a result.

And to make matters worse, the one-bedroom apartment I was promised was nothing more than a studio with a divider. When I complained to my daughter about the accommodations, she lapsed into her spiel again about all the wonderful activities Springtime Pastures offered and said she didn't think I'd be spending much time in my lovely little room anyway. And as much as I wanted to argue with her, she was right in a way. I was a natural extrovert, always the life of the party. I couldn't help the fact that people were drawn to my bubbly, feisty personality. We can't all be wallflowers, you know!

On a brighter note, there was a dining room downstairs, and three meals a day were included with the rent. Three meals a day of all-you-can-eat pureed crap. At least, that's what I told my daughter, as I laid into her with a little guilt for sticking me in a "home." Truthfully, though, the food wasn't all that bad, if a bit bland. Didn't these cooks here know that elderly taste buds needed a little extra help? *High blood pressure be damned*, I remember thinking, *give me some salt!*

It didn't take me long, however, to realize just how out of place I was here. Most of the residents of B-Block were easily in their eighties. I was only sixty-three. Okay, okay, I'm really sixty-seven. But I'm a young sixty-seven! And of course, the women greatly outnumbered the men here. To make matters worse, none of the few male residents were in any shape to have any fun with. So here I was, in the prime of my life and at my sexual peak, without any real prospects close at hand. I would have to venture farther out into the newer parts of the community for that.

You're probably wondering what happened to my daughter's father right about now. Well, the truth is, I have no idea. I never really knew for sure which of my lovers from back in the day had successfully impregnated me. There were so many possibilities! There was Randy, the cute but slightly stupid video store clerk who kept trying to hit the Play button even after my tape was already at its end for the evening; Bradley, the overly eager door-to-door insurance salesman who always got to the end of his sales pitch a smidge too quickly; Dean, the car mechanic who excelled at lube jobs but had trouble getting his own plug to spark; and Michael, the consumer product tester who kept trying to get me to rate his products. He was the most insecure of them all.

Since I didn't know who the father was, I ended up raising my daughter as a single mother, with a bit of help from my parents when she was younger. Once she was in school, I began working to save up for a down payment on a house of our own. I worked as a cashier in a grocery store, a personal shopper for an eccentric but wealthy widow, a teller at a bank, a masseuse—whatever I had to do to earn money. But it took me ten years to buy a house, which was why I still had a mortgage now and why I was presently at the mercy of my daughter and son-in-law.

Generally speaking, she and I were on pretty good terms most of the time, at least until she stuck me in a "home." But that apple couldn't have fallen farther from its tree. It was as if someone had yanked it from its branch and then thrown it halfway across the world. Goodness knows I tried to expose her to all that life has to offer, so how I managed to raise such a puritanical daughter was beyond me. I had dreamed for years of the day when she'd finally be old enough for the two of us together to enjoy the finer things in life. Like vacationing in a nudist commune. Or hitchhiking our way across the country with nothing more than the clothes on our backs just to see how far we could get. Or even attempting to seduce a couple of straightlaced, married politicians we didn't like and then ruin their careers for the fun of it! Sadly, that day never came.

But I figured I'd done my best as a parent, and she needed to find her own way in the world. And I had to admit I'd be more than a little tickled if one of her children ends up taking after their grandmother. My daughter's tightly scripted existence would come crashing down around her, and I hoped to live long enough to see that day come. And then I'd take her wayward child under my wing. But until that day arrived, all I could do was pray to Mother Nature to work her magic.

I had bigger fish to fry anyway. The reconstruction of my house was taking longer than expected, and I had at least another few weeks to go until it would be ready. Which meant another few weeks staying here at Springtime Pastures. It wasn't all bad, though. I managed to sneak in a hot plate and some cooking utensils, and unlike that lovable fictitious character from that '80s sitcom about four senior ladies in Miami, I managed *not* to burn down the retirement home when I used it. Or, at least, that's what she was accused of having done.

My adventures with two of the book clubs I tried out weren't as successful, however. I got kicked out of the first one for suggesting we read a steamy romance book. I got kicked out of the second one because the leader accused me of trying to seduce her husband. Right, like that was going to happen. He's ninety years old, out of his mind half the time, and still thinks the few hairs he has left on his head that he tries to comb over are a real badge of masculine virility. Thanks, but no thanks.

Since I had access to all of the community's amenities and wasn't confined to B-Block, I had taken up water aerobics at a pool in one of the newer areas. And it didn't hurt that the instructor was gorgeous. Absolutely gorgeous. His name was Scott. He was just my type. Lean, muscled, and thirty years my junior. He had made it all the way to the Olympics some years back, but he had suffered a pretty serious injury that ended his competitive swimming career. By the time he recovered, the profession had moved on from him. He was devastated, of course, but well, his loss was our gain. He was a damn good instructor, showing us how to stretch our limbs and muscles in the water without risk of injury. My only real gripe with him was that he refused to wear a Speedo, even after I gave him one for his birthday last month. I had to guess the size, of course, but I was pretty good at measuring with my eyes.

So imagine my surprise when I arrived for my water aerobics class earlier this morning to find Scott face down in the pool, dead as a doornail, *and* wearing a Speedo.

2

I was usually the first one to arrive for this particular water aerobics class. So, after checking my purse to make sure I didn't have anything in there that could get me arrested on a possession charge, I called for the emergency responders—you know, the police and the paramedics. I was pretty sure it was too late to try to revive Scott, given that he had already sunk to the bottom of the pool. But since I practiced in what you might call holistic medicine, I figured it would be best to let the traditional medical experts make that determination. You know, for accuracy's sake.

Unfortunately, and predictably, some of the other ladies in the class arrived before the emergency responders did. Lanie Sanders was first; she was always the second one here. A striking artificial brunette at five foot eight, she had one of those faces you'd be hard-pressed to forget: a pronounced jawline, beautifully capped white teeth, a perfectly proportioned nose, and eyes as green as emeralds. Despite being in her seventies, she had only the hints of crow's feet around those emeralds. She's one of those people that you love to hate. Always going on about her perfect life and her perfect marriage and her perfect children and her perfect house and her perfect breasts.

But I knew better. Her husband, who happened to be one of the few men around here who still looked like a man you'd want to sleep with, knew he was the rooster of roosters in the hen house and took full advantage of his fortune behind Lanie's back. I also knew that those children of hers were nothing but trouble. She and I went out for drinks one night shortly after I moved in, before I really got to know her, and after she'd put back a few, the truth came out. Her son was in prison for tax fraud, and her daughter had been in and out of mental institutions ever since she began seeing dead people. And those breasts Lanie was so proud of? I knew they weren't real. I may have accidentally copped a feel one day when we got a little too close to each other in the pool.

Anyway, before I had a chance to stop her, she jumped into the pool and began swimming toward where Scott's body lay. Unfortunately, she wasn't a very good swimmer. Oh sure, she could water-aerobic the hell out of her body, but swimming? No. It was a big pool, and he lay at the bottom of its center, so I watched her flail about for a couple of seconds, trying to suppress an overwhelming urge to laugh. About all she managed to do was splash water everywhere.

I ran over and retrieved an innertube that had a rope attached to it. Now I'm not usually the bragging type, but I was pretty good with a lasso back in my day, so I knew how to wrangle a target. And Lanie's head, in this particular instance, was the bull's-eye. After waiting a couple of seconds for her to take a break from flailing about, I threw the tube into the water and managed to land it directly over her head and onto her shoulders. She was stunned. Positively stunned. Especially after I started reeling her in with the rope.

"What are you doing?" she yelled at me as she tried to escape the confines of the tube. "We have to save Scott!"

"It's too late," I yelled back. "He was already at the bottom of the pool when I got here."

"But, but, but we can revive him! I know CPR!"

Well, of course I knew she knew CPR. Every time a man even hints that he might faint around here, she says she knows CPR. Every time a woman *actually* faints around here, she's nowhere to be found. I always thought the point of CPR was to save a life, not to see how many members of one particular sex you can kiss. Personally, I think she does it to try to make her husband jealous. Too bad Lanie doesn't realize that ship has already sailed, leaving her at the dock, frantically flapping her arms, trying to get her husband to pay attention to her.

Anyway, I explained to her again that once a body hits bottom, it's dead. Reluctantly, she stopped putting up a fight and allowed me to finish pulling her back toward the edge of the pool. I then stretched a hand to help her out, but she waved it away, muttering under her breath that she was in much better shape than I was and didn't need my help. Maybe she was right. She *was* in better shape, despite being nearly ten years older, but she couldn't swim worth a damn.

Lanie had better pray she and I never manage to find ourselves alone in a canoe in the middle of a lake. I'd be pretty tempted to capsize the boat, swim to shore myself, and then watch her slowly succumb to the murky waters. It's not that I despised Lanie. I just wished she'd mellow out a bit. I could help her with that if she'd let me, but knowing her, she'd probably turn me in. And then I'd get kicked out of Springtime Pastures and my daughter and son-in-law would have to take me in again. I don't know. Maybe it would be worth it in the end to see my daughter desperately trying everything she could to place me in another home. But then again, the next home might not be as hospitable as this one was, my little cell in B-Block notwithstanding.

"Millie," Lanie said as she regained her composure, "I'm holding you personally responsible for Scott's death. I could have saved him, you know. I know CPR!"

"Yes, you mentioned that. Just like I mentioned that he was already dead when I got here. As an aside, and I mean this out of genuine concern, you might want to have your doctor check your short-term memory."

"There's nothing wrong with my memory, you, you—"

She didn't have a chance to finish her insult because a third member of our class had arrived and made her presence known. Rebecca Stein was shorter than both Lanie and myself, at five foot two, and had a beautiful head of silvery hair that only nature could have created. She was made of good, sturdy Jewish stock and had a wit about her that I truly envied. Despite being a retired philosophy professor from one of those uptight ivy-league schools, she had a wicked sense of humor and a keen perception of the world around her and those who inhabited it.

"Such a shame," Rebecca said to the two of us as her eyes found Scott's body at the bottom of the pool. "But we never really know when it's our time to go, now do we? He was a handsome young man for sure. Has anybody called the authorities?"

I told her that I had and that there was nothing to do now but wait until they arrived. Lanie chimed in and told Rebecca that I had refused to allow her to save Scott's life, so I had to explain the whole situation to her from beginning to end, making sure to emphasize the futility and stupidity of Lanie's efforts. Lanie wasn't amused by my retelling of the preceding events, so she tried to retell the story while casting herself in a much more positive light. She made it sound like I simply stood there and watched Scott drown while she jumped in, risking her own life to save his. I could have decked her.

Fortunately, I could tell that Rebecca had seen right through Lanie's little fantasy by the quizzical-turned-reproachful expression on her face. Lanie, of course, didn't seem to notice. She's so damned self-absorbed that if I bit her, actually bit into her flesh right now, she wouldn't blink an eye. She'd just keep talking until she was done with what she had to say. Which is exactly what she did.

"Listen, Lanie," I said after she finally shut up, "I'll stay here until the authorities arrive, and Rebecca can go try to keep the rest of our class members from entering the pool area. There's really no need for you to stay, so why don't you go home to that beautiful husband of yours and that beautiful house of yours and then go stand in front of the mirror and admire those beautiful breasts of yours. We have things covered here."

"Why, thank you," she responded before thinking better of it. "Wait, no, someone needs to stay here and bear witness to what really happened."

"And that someone is going to be me," I said more assertively.

"Well, I'm not leaving!"

"Fine. Just don't get in my way," I said, hoping to end this little confrontation.

I don't mind being assertive when I have to be, but I much prefer to play the part of the slightly zany, often whimsical, and always mellow one in a group. It's my natural tendency. But Lanie Sanders was getting on my last nerve. And because she was getting on my last nerve, I hadn't noticed that a fourth member of our class had shown up.

Anna Lee Benton was the Deep South southerner among us. She had moved up here from Alabama to be closer to her children after her husband died. And she's every southern stereotype you've ever heard of wrapped up into one person. Always dressed well. Never wears flats, even here at the pool. She's got these wedge-shaped flip-flops she teeters around on. She's as sugary as sweet tea, but she'll bless your heart in an instant if you cross her. And if you know southerners, you know that's one of the worst insults you can receive from a true native.

"Oh, my word," Anna Lee said as she peered into the pool. "Whatever could have happened to that poor boy? Such a tragedy. So young. So virile."

Anna Lee fell somewhere in between Lanie and Rebecca in terms of her sensitivity to shock factors such as finding a dead body in the pool. She was clearly shaken, more so than Rebecca, but wasn't launching into hysterics like Lanie. She was a different kind of bird. She had never learned to drive. She was always driven. Always the queen bee of whatever social circle she happened to be traveling in at the time.

Even here at Springtime Pastures and now in her mid-eighties, she had managed to elevate her social standing, quickly climbing that ladder until she was satisfied with her position. Or at least, that's how Rebecca once described her to me. Lanie, as you can imagine, never could quite measure up to Anna Lee's status around here, and she was all the more jealous for it. Most people merely tolerated Lanie, but they genuinely admired Anna Lee. Except for me, that is. I've never had much use for pretentious belles. I grew up around enough of them to have had my fill several lifetimes over. But at least she didn't make me want to gouge her eyes out the way Lanie did.

"Millie," Anna Lee said, "Did you call the paramedics? I know it's probably too late, but someone is probably going to want to examine him."

"Yes, I did. But wait a sec. Why did you ask me? Why not Rebecca or Lanie?"

"Because, dear, you were the first one here. Weren't you? You're always the first one here. At least that's what Scott used to tell me when we'd have our little rendezvous."

"Rendezvous? You mean like when you fell down in your cottage, couldn't get up, and yet luckily had your cell phone in reach so you could call him for help? You know, you might want to consider getting one of those pendants you wear around your neck with a button you can press in such an emergency. Especially seeing as how Scott won't be paying anymore late-night visits to your cottage to peel you off the floor."

"I haven't the faintest clue what you're talking about," Anna Lee unconvincingly replied. "And how did you find out?"

"And while we're on the subject, how did you manage to convince Scott of all people to come to your rescue? He's not a member of the full-time staff here."

"You mean," Rebecca interjected, "that he *wasn't* a member of the full-time staff here. No sense in pretending he's still alive."

Lanie let out a faint whimper. I told her to get a grip. Rebecca told her to act her age. Anna Lee joked that her own fainting couch was in the shop, so Lanie had best do what she could to keep herself upright. I gave her bonus points for that admittedly witty remark. I wished we could have continued this little three-on-one gang up against Lanie, but I began to hear sirens in the background.

"Listen up," I said, "before the police and paramedics get here, I want to say emphatically that Scott was already at the bottom of the pool when I got here this morning."

"We believe you," Rebecca said.

"Speak for yourself," Lanie responded through the tears streaming down her face. "I have no reason to believe you, Millie. How long have we known you now? Less than six months? Why should we trust you? How do we know you didn't have something to do with this?"

"Because I'm telling you that I didn't," I snapped. "What motive could I possibly have had?"

"Well, dear," Anna Lee interjected in that lyrical drawl of hers, "now I'm not saying you have anything to worry about. But I did happen to notice the little Speedo still attached to Scott's body. We all know of your, um, persistent efforts to get him to wear one of those during our classes. So it's not that far-fetched to reckon that perhaps you showed up early this morning, held a gun to his head and told him to wear the Speedo or else. So, of course, he did. And then maybe there was something else you wanted him to do that he refused. You know, like sexual favors or something, and so you shot him."

I took a moment to look Anna Lee in the eye to see if she was joking. She wasn't.

"Don't you think that if I'd shot him, there'd be blood in the pool? And on the deck somewhere?" I asked, gobsmacked that I even had to point out something so obvious. "And since you were all there when I gave him a Speedo for his birthday last month, you also know that the Speedo he's wearing now is not the same Speedo I gave him then."

"But," Lanie interjected, launching into hysterics again, "that doesn't prove anything! You could have brought that one with you this morning. Before you shot him! Murderer!"

"Lanie," Rebecca said, "if you really believe that Millie killed Scott, then you'd have to also believe that she'd be capable of murdering any one of us as well, with whatever weapon she must have stowed somewhere on the premises before we all got here. So, it might not be such a wise idea for you to call attention to your suspicion that she is, indeed, a murderer. Or you might end up being her next victim."

That shut Lanie up, and she cowered behind Anna Lee, which was fine with me. I told them all that I, too, would like to know where Scott had gotten that Speedo, and then the police and the paramedics arrived.

3

After the police took our statements, we were asked to leave the premises. Rebecca and Anna Lee were pretty accurate in their description of the morning's events, but I had to correct Lanie on several points while she was giving hers. She really didn't do herself any favors, since she was contradicting much of what the rest of us had said. But the police dutifully took down her statement and said they'd be in touch with us if they had any further questions.

The paramedics knew as I had that there was no reviving Scott, so they left him in the pool and waited for a special team to retrieve him from where he lay. I had so desperately wanted to stick around, but because the police weren't sure yet whether there was any foul play involved, they deemed the pool a crime scene, and we had to leave. Would have been nice if I could have examined Scott up close for myself, to see if there were any visible clues as to the cause of his death, of course, but that was out of the question. He was probably stiff by now in all the wrong places anyway.

I got back to my little cell in B-Block, unsure of what to do next. I mean, it's not every day you go to your water aerobics class and find your instructor face down in the pool. So, rather than stew around my room, I went downstairs to see if I could find Julie. I figured she'd want to know of Scott's death since they were, as she once put it, friends with benefits. Or at least that's what she wanted me to believe. And who could blame her? He was gorgeous, and she was lonely. I'm sure sleeping with him would have been a badge of honor for her. Even pretending to have slept with him probably gave her ego a boost.

Julie von Haffen was an odd duck, if ever there was one. I had gotten to know her better than I would have liked to over these last six months. She was most definitely not a friend of Mary and Jane, so I had to be really careful around her. She was always threatening me with random inspections of my cell. But she did it with a smile on her face every time. Like I was some sort of child hiding candy in my room. Julie was no match for me, though, as I always made sure I stayed one step ahead of her.

Early on in my stay here, I made the mistake of trying to get to know her better, and she spilled her whole life's story to me. Born to devoutly religious parents in a small town just outside Wichita, Kansas, she was practically groomed from birth to become a devoted wife and fertile mother. She had told me her parents wanted her to have at least ten children, and she herself was the youngest of eight. Now, I knew that parents generally wanted their children to have more than they had, but usually it's in reference to money, careers, and possessions. Not more children!

Well, Julie had other plans for her life, so when she graduated high school, she split and never looked back. The way she tells it, she went wild. Kind of like those Amish kids who partake in Rumspringa do when they have their two years to explore the world outside their communities. She tasted every Skittle in the rainbow, as they say, and had a blast doing it too. But like the Amish kids who choose to return to their communities, she settled back down eventually, though she never did return home. When I asked her why she was so averse now to the pleasures that Mary and Jane had to offer, she recounted a tragic story of love and loss involving a guy she had been seeing who had overdosed on the hard stuff. So, I suppose I couldn't blame her for her attitude, but it certainly put a crimp in my style!

She made up for that in other ways, though. It was Julie who had suggested I join the water aerobics class in the first place. I was hesitant in the beginning, but when she described Scott in vivid detail, well, I couldn't resist. Everyone needs a little eye candy now and then, and since my options at Springtime Pastures were few and far between, I figured I had better get my visual kicks where I could. And Scott certainly didn't disappoint.

"I can't believe it. I don't want to believe it," Julie said after I broke the news of his death to her. "I don't know what I'm going to do without my Scotty."

"I know, I know," I said, trying to console her. "It was a shock to all of us. I was the one who found him and had to call the authorities. And then three of the other ladies showed up before they arrived. It was a circus. One of them nearly accused me of killing him."

Julie's eyes widened a bit, so I assured her that, no, he was completely dead before I showed up and that I was certain there was no chance of resuscitating him. And then she did something that caught me by surprise. She started rubbing her stomach.

"Oh no," I said. "Please don't tell me—"

"It's true."

"How far along are you?" I asked, not completely convinced yet that she was truly pregnant.

"Three months."

"Did Scott know?"

He hadn't known, and maybe that was a blessing. Who knows? Maybe she was making this pregnancy up. For all I knew, she was psychotic and had dreamed up this whole fantasy about having any sort of relationship with him. But for the time being, I decided to keep my suspicions to myself. Like I said before, Julie's an odd duck, and she lives in her own special brand of reality.

She asked me if I thought we should plan some sort of memorial gathering in his honor for the residents at Springtime Pastures who knew him. I told her that I thought it was a nice idea but that we should probably wait a bit to see what his family was going to do before we planned anything. I seemed to recall him mentioning that his parents and siblings lived out of town somewhere, wherever he was from. I was drawing a blank on that last detail, but Julie reminded me that he was from Connecticut. Stamford, to be exact.

"Listen," I said, circling back to the bun in Julie's oven. "Perhaps you shouldn't tell anyone else about your condition. At least not for a while. Let the dust settle a bit. How long had you really been seeing Scott, anyway? Do his parents know about you? It would come as quite a shock if you reached out to let them know they had a grandchild on the way if they didn't even know of your existence."

"I think they know about me, about us, but I'm not sure. I asked him to tell them. He said he would. We were getting pretty serious," she said as a tear ran down her cheek. "I wanted to meet them, but they haven't been down for a visit in a while."

"Or at least that's what he told you," I added. "For all you know, they might have been here, and he didn't tell you. Maybe he wasn't ready for you to meet them? Maybe he wasn't on the same page as you were about your relationship."

"You're probably right. I know I have a bigger-than-life personality," she said in a rare moment of candor. "But it's like, why be anything else? Life's a brunch and most poor suckers are starving to death. Maybe he thought I'd be too much for his parents to handle."

I was pretty sure she had messed up a word from that famous movie expression, but I didn't correct her. Brunch or banquet, it didn't matter in the end.

"You just, well, you're an acquired taste. That's all. If you're ever interested, I might be able to procure something that'll mellow you out a bit."

For a moment, she looked interested, but then the light bulb in that blond head of hers turned on, and she realized what I was referring to. A slight grimace soon followed.

"Okay," I continued. "I won't mention it again. But let me ask you this. Did anyone else know about you and Scott? It's not every day that a perfectly healthy male specimen like Scott is discovered face down in a pool. People are going to start asking questions. Like, who would have had a motive to kill him? Did he have any enemies? Of course, he may have had an underlying health condition that not even he knew about."

"Wait, are you saying someone might think I did it?" she asked in genuine surprise. "I wouldn't hurt a fly."

"You didn't answer my question, dear. Who else knew about you and Scott besides me? None of the other members residing here in B-Block are in our water aerobics class. And to the best of my knowledge, no one here would have had any reason to have any contact with him. But that doesn't mean there aren't others in the greater community you might have confided in."

I knew I was grasping at straws here. Even if Julie had told others about her alleged relationship with Scott, I doubted anyone would believe her capable of killing him. But, well, I kind of enjoyed seeing her squirm in her seat a bit. Served her right for keeping too close an eye on me and my medicinal habits.

"Well," she said, "I might have told some of the other activities directors about Scott and me. I couldn't help myself! I was so happy!"

And then the tears started flowing uncontrollably. Whatever this was, they were clearly more than friends with benefits in her eyes. I told her to pull herself together before someone overheard. We were in her office, but the door was wide open, and if there's one thing you can be sure of in a retirement home, it's that you can barely keep yourself from tripping over a nosy busybody. They're everywhere here! Most of the residents in B-Block didn't have much going on in their own lives, so they were particularly keen on the goings on of others. Especially of those who lived on the outside.

She grabbed a tissue from the tissue box on her desk, wiped away some of the tears, and then blew her nose so loudly she could have woken the dead. *How unattractive,* I thought. I tell you, it's like she has to do everything bigger and better than anyone else. I was about to get out of my seat and walk around to her side of the desk to console her when one of the aforementioned busybodies walked in on us.

"It's time for bingo! We're waiting!" the busybody said.

I didn't know this particular lady. Sure, I had seen her around in the dining room, but I hadn't made an effort to socialize with her. Sometimes I get these feelings about people, like warning signs telling me to stay away. You know what I mean? Her aura was very off-putting to me, lots of crazy energy emanating from her being. Plus, she was decked out from head to toe in sequins. Like, "Everyone had better pay attention to me because I'm hot shit," or perhaps, "I can't see worth a damn anymore, so I have no idea how ridiculous I really look." And it didn't even seem to register with her that Julie was having some sort of meltdown. She couldn't have cared less. Even Lanie wasn't this bad.

Having taken another tissue from the box, Julie wiped away the rest of her tears and told the busybody she'd be there in a minute and to let the other bingo players know as well. The sequined busybody looked none too happy about being given the brush-off but obliged and left the office.

"Millie," Julie said, "I know bingo isn't your thing, but I could really use some moral support out there today. Could I convince you to play? I could use a friendly face in the audience. I'm not sure I can hold it together long enough to call even a single number. Oh, maybe you could do it for me! It's not hard!"

"Let me get this straight. You want *me* to run your bingo game?" I asked. "What would I get in return for doing this favor for you?"

"But I thought we were friends, you and me. Friends do things like this for each other. Like run bingo games."

"No dice," I said. "I want something tangible in return. And where in the hell did you get the idea that we were friends? I think I made it pretty clear when I moved in here that you had to, um, meet a certain bar to be granted entrance into my circle of friends. You didn't meet said bar, so we're merely acquaintances."

She looked hurt, and I ever so slightly regretted what I had just said. Truth be told, we had, indeed, become friends, at least on some level. We didn't socialize together, of course, but I had to give her credit for helping me to adapt to living in a "home." And she did more than what was simply required of her position. Julie had given me the inside scoop on the various staff members who worked in B-Block, as well as those who worked elsewhere in the community. She gave me pointers on who genuinely cared about the residents and who was simply in this line of work for the meager paycheck. And from my experiences over these last six months, her assessments were spot on. Oh, she looked like she had a few screws loose, and her demeanor didn't do her any favors in this regard either, but she was a good judge of character.

"Listen," I said as she melted into another puddle of tears, "I didn't mean that. We are friends. You've been mostly good to me, and I'm grateful for that. So, let's pull ourselves together now and go face the bingo players."

"Do you really mean it?" Julie asked, genuinely surprised at my change in tune.

"Yes, but we better go quickly before I change my mind."

She snapped to like she hadn't a care in the world, leaving me to wonder if she had some sort of ability to summon tears on command. Like maybe she wasn't as broken up as she had seemed a moment ago. I'd have to keep an eye on her and possibly be a little more vigilant going forward. The last thing I wanted was someone on the inside who thought she could manipulate me. I didn't need anyone thinking I was a sucker for a sob story and then trying to make me her bitch.

Anyway, we walked out of her office and down the hall toward the B-Block activity room, a drab space with linoleum flooring and harsh florescent lighting. I understood the need for flooring that could be sanitized in a jiffy. No telling how many residents here had incontinence issues. But the lighting, well, it didn't do the ancient faces around here any favors. And the furniture was also easy to clean. Hard tables and hard chairs. While I didn't have this particular problem myself, yet, the interior decorators here failed to understand that old butts are bony and need a little cushion.

"Everyone! Can I have your attention?" Julie asked, very loudly and very slowly. "We have a very special guest today! Millie Holt is going to be our host for today's bingo game! Everyone give her a round of applause!"

4

The bingo game was a bust. The sequined busybody kept yelling "Bingo" when she didn't actually have a bingo. Another lady thought we were playing gin rummy and had to be told several times that "No, we are playing bingo." A third kept asking me to repeat the numbers I was calling because she had forgotten to put her hearing aids in before she left her cell. And a fourth got perilously close to setting her bingo card on fire with her cigarette lighter several times. The whole experience gave me a newfound respect for Julie.

Or at least it would have if she had managed to hold herself together. But no, she broke down several times crying out for her Scotty, so of course, then everyone wanted to know who Scotty was and what had happened to him. Despite my best efforts earlier in advising her to keep her mouth shut about their alleged romance, the cat was out of the bag. She told everyone within earshot that she had just lost the love of her life, the father of her child, and the best man she ever knew. And I had to admit, Julie put on a pretty good performance, so perhaps no one would ever suspect her of having anything to do with Scott's death in the end. I mean, she was obviously grief-stricken.

Why she felt the need to inform everyone that I had been the one to find his dead body, I didn't know. But I wasn't too thrilled with the attention I was receiving as a result. Everyone wanted all of the details. What time had I found him? Where had I found him? Did I see anyone else near the site of his death?

After the bingo game was over, we went back into her office, and I did my best to console her. Not an easy task. I told her that if I could gain access to an oven, I'd be happy to bake her up a batch of brownies to lift her spirits, making no mention of a particular ingredient I had intended to use, of course. But she declined, saying that since she was eating for two, she wanted only the best for her baby. Well, that proved it, I suppose. She really was pregnant. No one in their right mind would ever turn down homemade brownies, even without my special ingredient added in for good measure.

Anyway, I had just gotten back to my room, feeling pretty exhausted by the day's events, and begun to undress when my cell phone rang. I didn't recognize the number, but figured I had nothing left to lose today, so I answered the call.

"Hello. This is Anna Lee Benton calling for a Ms. Millie Holt. Is she available to speak with me?"

"Oh, hello, Anna Lee," I responded. "To what do I owe the pleasure of your call?"

I didn't know how she had my number, as I clearly didn't know hers and didn't want to know hers. I couldn't say that she was ever overtly rude to me, but she made it known in her own way that I was beneath her social status. And I was perfectly fine with that, so why she was calling now I had no idea.

"I'm having one of my afternoon tea socials in about an hour, and I was calling to see if you might grace us with your presence? I know I could use a little cheering up right now, and I'm betting you could too. The tragic events of this morning have really put a damper on my mood, and I thought perhaps you might regale us with some of your, um, stories of your fascinating life."

Anna Lee was laying it on pretty thick. She never cared about me or my life before. Why should it be any different now? And she's never invited me to one of her afternoon teas before, not that I would have gone if she had. No, something was up here. Something fishy. I couldn't quite put my finger on it, though. I needed more information.

"Listen, Anna Lee, let's cut right to the chase. Why now, after all these months, have you decided that I'm worthy enough to make an appearance at one of your overhyped social functions, let alone even letting me set foot inside your cottage?"

She was taken aback by my bluntness, but recovered quickly.

"I just thought it would be helpful to, um, go over today's events among those of us who witnessed them. Rebecca and Lanie have already agreed to come, so you're the last holdout at this point. And take my word for it, you don't want to be the last holdout for this particular occasion. Think for a moment about what Lanie was alluding to earlier, about your possible involvement in Scott's untimely passing. Think long and hard about that before you decline my gracious invitation."

I had no desire to rehash my discovery of Scott's dead body in the pool any further, and certainly not with the three of them, but she had a point. If they were indeed going to discuss what had transpired, then I damn sure was going to be there to defend myself against any additional accusations Lanie planned on making against me. And I supposed I wouldn't mind listening to what Rebecca had to say on the matter. Like I said before, she was a retired philosophy professor and was pretty adept at reasoning through difficult situations with pure logic.

"I see your point, Anna Lee," I responded. "I think you're all getting ahead of yourselves here since for all we know, he could have had a pre-existing health condition. But I'll be there, if only to shut Lanie up. Can I bring anything for this tea social of yours? Want to make it a high tea?"

She didn't get the joke.

"No need to bring anything. Just yourself. Now normally, I do ask the women to dress up a bit for my afternoon teas, but I don't expect it of you. And since it'll only be the four of us, and since we've all seen each other in our bathing suits anyway, I figure there's no sense in adhering to formalities today. Come as you are. And should today's tea go well, you could be looking forward to further invitations!"

I wanted to tell her what she could do with her further invitations, and maybe I would do precisely that on the day I finally move back into my own home, but for now I held my tongue.

"Thank you, Anna Lee," I said. "Do you require me to wear a shirt? Or are tops optional for this little shindig of yours? Because you said I should come as I am, and right now I'm topless."

"What?!"

"Just a little joke," I reassured her. "I'll be there, fully clothed."

"I'm so looking forward to your presence here," she said unconvincingly. "We're going to start at 3:00 p.m. Do you have the address? Do you need directions from B-Block? Or if you'd like, I can send my driver to come pick you up. Give you a chance to ride in the lap of luxury for a change. That trusty old Toyota of yours has surely seen better days."

I wasn't sure whether Anna Lee was offering to have me chauffeured out of true generosity or because she didn't want any of her neighbors to see my dented-up car parked in her driveway. On the one hand, I wouldn't mind a ride in her cushy S-Class Mercedes. Maybe I'd leave a little present of some sort for her in the backseat. Something I knew would ruffle her feathers a bit. But on the other hand, it would mean being at her mercy should I wish to leave before she wanted me to. And I didn't like the sound of that.

"No, thank you," I said. "I'll drive myself, and if you'd like, I'll park a block away so I don't crowd your driveway with my car. That'll leave more room for Rebecca and Lanie to park theirs. And since I'm the youngest of the group, walking a block or two is far easier for me than it is for them."

I didn't mean to throw Rebecca under the bus like that, but I didn't mind chucking Lanie to the curb. Or better yet, dumping her out in the middle of the street and then running over her at high speed.

"Lovely idea, and so generous of you to think of the others," Anna Lee responded. "Well, then, I reckon I'll see you at three. I'll text you the address as soon as we end this call."

She ended the call before I could get another word in, and sure enough, I had a text message from her not five minutes later. Now that I had her phone number, I wondered if maybe I should sign her up for some online marketing websites. I could make up a phony email address, of course, but I knew her name, address, and phone number, and that was going to be enough to set some of those nasty little telemarketers on her case.

I could sign her up for incontinence product info calls or perhaps some sort of male escort service. Maybe I could even get someone to call her up and whisper lewd comments about how much he desired her and that he wanted to meet her and sex her up but was in prison on a murder charge. You're probably thinking I should at least give her some credit for being gracious, whatever her true motivations might have been. And that's fine. But where's the fun in that?

I mulled over the bit from our conversation when she said, "Come as you are." But I knew her well enough to know she didn't really mean that and only said it in an attempt to remove a potential obstacle to my showing up. She probably thought a woman like me didn't have anything nice to wear. And given that I lost most of my worldly possessions in the fire, she probably would have been right. But I did have one outfit that I was pretty sure was nice enough even for Anna Lee's discerning tastes.

A couple of months ago, my son-in-law made partner at his law firm, and there was a big ceremony and celebration. I had no desire to attend, still fuming over my current living arrangement, but I had little choice in the matter. Again, here's where the whole "not having the upper hand" situation really hurt me. I felt as if I were a puppet and they were the puppet masters, pulling my strings every which way they pleased. So I had to show up, which meant I had to have a suitable outfit to wear.

Anyway, my daughter picked me up at B-Block a few days before the big shindig and took me shopping for, as she put it, "a respectable suit for the mother-in-law of the newest partner at the most prestigious law firm in the Triangle area" to wear. She wanted me to look the part, never mind the fact that I had no interest in playing this particular role. She took me to Saks and bought me a navy blue, skirted single-breasted suit, a cream-colored blouse to wear underneath, and matching navy-blue two-inch heels. I hated heels and hadn't worn a pair since my daughter's wedding ten years ago. And even then, my daughter practically forced me into them. Oh, and she bought me a very expensive pearl necklace to wear, as well.

She also insisted that, on the morning of the big day at the law-firm, I ride over to her house so she could do my hair and makeup, not trusting me to fashion a presentable appearance on my own. And perhaps she was right, because I would never have dolled myself up the way she had done. When she was through, I really did look the part of a respectable, high-society mother-in-law. I hated every minute of it, and I made sure she knew it. But again, what choice did I have except to cooperate? I did, however, do a little "hoot and holler" routine when my son-in-law's promotion to partner was officially announced at the ceremony. My daughter was mortified, and my son-in-law looked at me as if nonverbally communicating to the other partners that he had no idea who I was.

I opened my closet and stared at the suit and blouse, still in their clear plastic bags from the dry cleaners and wondered whether it was really worth the fuss to dress for Anna Lee's tea social. I could wear the jacket, a white T-shirt underneath, and perhaps a pair of slacks. The problem with this plan, though, was that the only white T-shirts I had contained lettering and/or graphics that would probably set Anna Lee's hair on fire. I had one with the words *Pot Granny* in big green letters. Another displayed an image of two scantily clad men in an embrace, with the words *Love Is Love* beneath. A third showed a raised middle finger and the words *Screw the*

Government below. And a fourth had an image of a Black Jesus.

In the end, I decided to wear the damn suit. And after fixing myself a small lunch, not wanting to bother with a trip to the dining room downstairs, I got dressed and even put on the heels and pearls for good measure. When I looked myself over in the mirror, however, I realized pretty quickly that something was missing. No makeup, and no makeup products to apply either. My daughter threw away what little I had brought with me to her house before that shindig, and I hadn't bothered to replace any of it. I thought I looked all right without makeup, but I figured that if I was going to play dress up for Anna Lee's tea social, I probably should go all the way.

Grabbing my pocketbook from the counter, I walked out of my cell and made my way downstairs in search of Julie. I knew she'd be all too thrilled to help me in my hour of need. Plus, she owed me big time for that fiasco of a bingo game earlier. I found her seated behind the desk in her office, dabbing away at the tears flowing from her eyes again. Rather than ask her if she was okay, when she clearly wasn't, I told her that I needed her help with something that I knew would lift her spirits.

"I'm so sad," she said in response. "I can't believe I lost my Scotty. I'm too young to be a widow."

"Julie, in order to be a widow, you would need to have been married first," I pointed out.

"Oh, well, I guess I'm not a widow then. But I feel like one. Doesn't that count for something?"

"Um, I'm sure it does, but listen. I need you to do my makeup for me. I've been invited to one of Anna Lee Benton's socials, and I want to look my best."

It was then that Julie realized I was dressed to the nines and ready to impress. The tears stopped flowing, and a smile began to spread across her face.

"Oh, my goodness! We're going to have such fun! I've been wanting to get my hands on your face ever since you moved in!"

"Yes, I know. Well, now's your chance. Don't blow it. Make me look like a rich bitch!"

She had a whole desk drawer full of makeup products and began pulling out bottles, powders, applicators, lipsticks, and several shades of nail polish. I told her I didn't have time for the polish, but that everything else was fair game. And in the end, she made me up beautifully. Not my style of course, but she had succeeded in giving me the face of an aristocratic old broad with an attitude. Exactly what I wanted or, rather, what I knew would impress Anna Lee.

5

I drove to Anna Lee's cottage a short while later, managing to find it with no trouble at all. It just so happened that one of those few male residents who still looked like someone you'd want to sleep with lived around the corner, and I had been keeping an eye on him for a while, waiting to make my move. He was a widower, having lost his wife several months ago to a short illness, and as far as I was concerned, he'd been in mourning long enough and was thus fair game.

Pulling into Anna Lee's driveway, I nearly forgot about my earlier plan to park a block away and walk back. But after taking one look at my feet scrunched into these heels, I decided she'd have to live with my beat-up old Toyota parked in her driveway for one blessed afternoon. If she wanted me here badly enough, then she could deal with the shame and embarrassment my car brought to the otherwise charming picture her front yard presented.

I rang the doorbell, and a woman whom I didn't know answered the door. Figures. She had a maid. Of course, she had a maid. No queen bee in her right mind would go a day without proper domestic help. Even if said bee lived in a one-bedroom cottage that couldn't have been more than a thousand square feet in size. Anyway, I introduced myself, and the maid led me inside to the living room where the other ladies were already seated and enjoying some refreshments. They all looked at me in wonder and astonishment, not having ever seen me in such formal attire.

"Well, look at you, my dear," Anna Lee said. "You're looking positively radiant. The suit really, um, suits you. I'm so glad you decided to join us."

I should note here that none of the other ladies were dressed for the occasion, so I felt a bit awkward and out of place. Especially in this getup that was so not my style. Anna Lee was wearing taupe slacks with a turquoise sweater set on top. Rebecca was in jeans and a white, loosely fitting men's button-down dress shirt. And Lanie was in a pair of capri pants and a floral-patterned T-shirt.

"I always dress to impress," I lied, which elicited a chuckle from Lanie and a knowing glance from the other two.

I took a seat on the sofa next to Rebecca, with Lanie and Anna Lee both in armchairs at opposite ends. The coffee table was spread with several varieties of finger food, some of which I recognized and some of which I dared not try. A pitcher of tea, sweet no doubt, and a pitcher of lemonade with actual slices of lemon bobbing around were strategically placed to balance out the display. Thankfully, none of us was a diabetic, as far as I knew.

"Well, now that we're all here," Anna Lee continued, "I thought it would be a nice idea for us to talk about what happened to poor Scott earlier today. The whole mess isn't sitting right with me. As you all know, Scott and I were fairly close, and I'm positively sure that if he'd had a health condition that would have caused sudden death, he would have told me."

"You're not fooling anyone," Rebecca said. "I don't believe for one minute that you were any closer to Scott than the rest of us. I know you're upset. We're all upset. But stop the embellishments, please."

"But it's how we do things down here," Anna Lee explained. "Sometimes you have to sugarcoat the truth a bit to make it more palatable. It's like me telling Millie a moment ago that her suit really suited her. It doesn't. In fact, it looks downright awkward on her. But we don't say such things out loud down here."

"No, you just say it behind someone's back," Rebecca added.

I was getting a little peeved here. I put all that effort into dolling myself up for these hens, and this was the thanks I was getting for it. I had half a mind to walk right back out through the door from which I came.

"Exactly, dear," Anna Lee said. "No sense in hurting someone's feelings to their face. That's bordering on cruel."

"No. Trashing someone behind their backs is cruel. If you have a problem with someone, you should just come right out and say it. But let's get back to you and Scott. Why the need to embellish a friendship with him? Or perhaps make one up out of thin air? You've got plenty of friends here at Springtime Pastures, so it can't be that you're lonely."

"Well, he made me feel like a woman. Always flirting with me. Telling me what an exquisite specimen of a woman I was."

"Honey," Rebecca continued, "when a thirty-something-year-old man tells an eighty-five-year-old woman that she's beautiful, he's doing it out of kindness, not lust. You never had a chance with him, and there's no sense in living in a fantasy world. He never saw you as a MILF."

"And what exactly do you mean by MILF?" Anna Lee asked.

I was wondering myself. I'm usually pretty caught up on the latest lingo, but I had to admit this one stumped me.

"MILF stands for 'Mother I'd Like to Fuck'," Rebecca informed us, which horrified Lanie and nearly sent Anna Lee into cardiac arrest.

"All right," I interjected. "I've had just about enough of all of this. Look, I came here against my better judgment to discuss what happened to Scott. I don't care whether Anna Lee slept with Scott or tried to sleep with Scott or merely fantasized about sleeping with Scott. Hell, we've all fantasized about sleeping with Scott at one point or another. And don't any of you try to deny it. I know better. Especially you, Lanie."

Lanie looked aghast at my calling her out in particular, but I knew she had it bad for him. Subtlety wasn't her forte, and I couldn't begin to count the number of times I caught her staring at him before, during, and after our water aerobics classes. Come to think of it, maybe I could use that to my advantage here. Think about it. Lanie was so quick to accuse me of having something to do with his death. But maybe, just maybe, it was her. I mean, doesn't a guilty party usually try to point the accusatory finger in someone else's direction?

"I don't know what you're talking about, Millie," Lanie responded. "But you've gone too far this time. You really have. Why would I risk my perfect marriage for a fling with a pool boy?"

"Because," Rebecca interjected, "your marriage isn't so perfect. It's taken me months to try to decide if you're willfully naïve or simply naturally so. I'm going with the latter. You're just stupid."

"Well, of all the nerve!" Lanie yelled as she got up out of her seat, intending to make a grand exit.

"Sit back down, dear," Anna Lee said. "No sense in pretending to be offended. She's simply trying to get a rise out of you, and you're letting her. She is right about your marriage, though. It could use a little work."

"And besides," I said to Lanie, "I only accused you of *fantasizing* about sleeping with Scott. I wasn't suggesting you were actually planning on trying."

Lanie sat back down and, in what can only be described as an epic pouting session, refused to look any of the rest of us in the eye.

"All right now," I continued. "Let's have a show of hands. Who here thinks Scott died of natural causes?"

No one raised her hand.

"Who here thinks Scott was murdered?"

All three of the ladies raised their hands. I still had no reason to believe he was killed, but I figured I had better let this play out, for now.

"Who here thinks I killed Scott?"

Lanie started to raise her hand, but Rebecca gave her such a disapproving stare that her hand only made it halfway up before she began lowering it again.

"So, does anyone have any suggestions as to how Scott was killed or who killed him and why?"

By this point, I was merely placating the others. I still didn't believe Scott was murdered. And as much as I wanted to believe Lanie had indeed done so, simply because I despised her, I knew she wasn't capable of it. None of us were, as far as I was concerned. None of us had any real motive to kill him, and none of us were crazy enough to kill him for no good reason. So, either Scott died of natural causes, or he was murdered by someone not presently in this room.

"All right," I continued after no one offered any suggestions, "let's say he was, indeed, murdered. Since the three of you are still stuck on this, how about a suggestion for a murder weapon? Remember, there was no visible blood in the pool or on the pool deck."

"Someone could have cleaned the deck before we all got there," Anna Lee suggested.

"Perhaps," Rebecca added, "but if there was blood on the deck, there would have been blood in the pool surrounding Scott's body."

"Not necessarily," I said. "Someone could have shot him and then plugged up the bullet hole. And if he was shot from the front, we wouldn't have seen it since he was face down by the time we got there."

"But don't bullets usually have an exit point as well?" Rebecca asked. "I suppose we don't know from what distance he was shot, but if it was at close range, that bullet would have torn right through him."

I reminded them all that we had no reason yet to believe Scott was shot, while silently chastising myself for adding fuel to this particular fire. But I figured Rebecca was probably right. If Scott had been shot at close range, there would have been an entry point and an exit point. There was no way someone could have plugged both ends up enough to stop the blood from seeping into the pool water. Or at least, that was my assumption. Hell, I'm no expert at this stuff. I could be way off here.

"Let's operate under the assumption that he wasn't shot," I continued. "There isn't any evidence to support the contrary, so then how? How was he murdered? What possible weapon could someone have used?"

"Well, isn't it obvious?" Lanie rhetorically asked. "Someone poisoned him."

"Or perhaps someone hit him over the head with a cast-iron skillet," Anna Lee suggested. "It's been known to happen before. The blow would have at least knocked him unconscious, and then the murderer probably pushed him into the pool, where he drowned."

A mental picture of some deranged soul bringing a cast-iron skillet to a pool for the express purpose of offing someone began to form in my mind, but it wasn't very convincing. Any number of more convenient objects could have been used to inflict a blunt force trauma. A brick, for example, and there was, indeed, a construction site near the pool. Springtime Pastures was erecting a new multipurpose auditorium, and you guessed it, the exterior was made of brick. It would have been all too easy for Scott's murderer to pilfer a brick from the site.

"He might have been strangled and then dumped in the pool," Rebecca said. "Maybe he had some enemies none of us knew about. Maybe some debts he had to pay, like to a loan shark or a mob boss. When he couldn't pay, some goon showed up, strangled him, and then dumped his body in the pool."

I asked Rebecca if she thought a hit man would have forced Scott into that Speedo before killing him, to which she responded that perhaps the hit man was gay and wanted maximal eye candy exposure before doing the deed. I supposed it wasn't out of the realm of possibility, but I did inform her that the mob wasn't particularly active around these parts of North Carolina. Loan sharks, however, were everywhere, and I had to admit that none of us really knew anything about Scott's personal financial situation.

"Maybe he was already in that Speedo when he arrived at the pool," Lanie said.

"A very real possibility," I added. "We don't really know what Scott's morning routine was before we all showed up for class each day. Maybe he did laps in the pool in said Speedo before we ever got there, and maybe he usually had time to change out of it before we'd have the chance to, umm, check out his package."

"For all we know, the Speedo had nothing to do with it," Rebecca concluded.

She was right, but I wasn't convinced yet. I believed Scott genuinely didn't like wearing Speedos anymore and wouldn't have put one on voluntarily this morning or any other morning.

"So, where the hell does this leave us?" Lanie asked in frustration.

"Oh, I believe we're still stuck at square one," Anna Lee said. "Seems to me that we've managed to come up with several, um, inventive ways for Scott to have met his Maker. And we could probably generate a laundry list of possible suspects or at least suspect types."

Rebecca added that she thought we needed to learn more about Scott's personal life and that, until we did, we might as well be grasping at air in our attempts to make sense of his murder.

"And how do you suggest we do that?" Lanie asked, barely concealing her skepticism that we'd be able to make any connection whatsoever.

"I think I might be able to help with that," I said to everyone's surprise.

So, of course I told them all about Julie von Haffen, since I was pretty sure none of them knew her. I mentioned Julie's alleged romance with him and that she claimed to be carrying his child. And then I mentioned how Julie had pretty much fallen apart after I broke the news of Scott's untimely death.

"Perhaps she might have a key to his house or apartment," Rebecca suggested. "We'd be able to look around and see if he left any clues as to who his assailant might have been. And since the murder took place at the pool and not his domicile, we wouldn't be disturbing a crime scene."

I was a little taken aback by her suggestion that we should actually investigate Scott's death. It was one thing for us to sit around here, letting our imaginations run wild as to how and why Scott was killed and by whom. It was another thing entirely for us to start talking about investigating our suspicions.

"I'll admit I don't know all of you as well as I probably should before asking this next question. But, well, here goes. Do any of you have any sort of background in criminal investigations?"

No one answered.

"That's what I thought," I continued. "And neither do I. So how about we leave the investigation to the professionals?"

"Even professionals miss things," Lanie responded, surprising me. "My Botox specialist missed an injection site once, and well, one side of my face looked about ten years older than the other until I could get it corrected. I didn't realize it until I got home that day, or I would have insisted she fix her sloppy work on the spot."

I supposed that explained the mere hints of crow's feet around her eyes. I wondered if, since she was being open about her Botox injections, she'd ever admit to having that boob job.

"So will you ask Julie about getting into Scott's home?" Rebecca asked.

"Do I have a choice?"

"I'm afraid, dear, that you're outnumbered here," Anna Lee said. "Oh, and would you mind asking her if he had any preexisting conditions while you're at it?"

6

By the time I got back to B-Block, Julie had already gone for the day. It was just as well. I was tired and in no mood to console the bereft, possibly-soon-to-be-future widow. I mean, she wasn't married to Scott, but if she had been, well you get my drift. I kicked off my heels, nearly tore the suit jacket as I undressed, and bent down on my knees to reach under the bed for my bottle of wine. I still don't understand why this damn place insists on a ban on alcohol in the residents' private cells. But since it does, I'm reduced to stashing my booze underneath my bed. How Julie hadn't caught on yet, I didn't know, but I was ever so thankful for her oversight in moments like this.

Another peculiarity at Springtime Pastures is that they don't like residents to have any sharp objects in their possession. Nothing sharper than a butter knife. Corkscrews were not allowed, so I had to buy my wine in bottles with screw caps.

And since I was by myself in my cell, I didn't bother with glasses. Just drank straight from the bottle and then screwed the cap on again when I was done. No fuss, no mess, no evidence. A flask would probably be more convenient for when I needed a quick swig, but having another container around doubled my chances of getting caught.

I thought about eating in tonight, ordering a meal to be delivered to my cell, but I've tried room service several times before, and in each instance my food arrived cold. Sure, they bring it in those covered dishes like the ones you see in hospitals for the inpatients, but somehow they never manage to get the food on the plate and covered up in time. If I didn't know any better, I'd suggest it was some sort of conspiracy against the residents here. Like, *if you want a hot meal, you better come down to the dining room to get it, because if you force us to put in the effort of bringing your food to you, we're going to do everything we can to make it a miserable experience for you so you never order room service again.*

After putting on a pair of jeans and one of my white T-shirts, the one with the "Pot Granny" wording, I reluctantly made my way down to the dining room. Sometimes, if I was lucky, I'd be able to snag a table for myself and then use my powerful nonverbal communication skills to deter others from sitting with me. Like pretending to have a cold by incessantly fake sneezing into a tissue. Or playing a prerecorded flatulence track on my phone. It's not that I didn't like people. I'm a natural extrovert. I simply hadn't found any residents here in B-Block who were capable of keeping a conversation going with me. I can only take so much of "Got me some new top-of-the-line dentures; corn on the cob here I come" or "I wonder if this food will require me to sleep on the toilet tonight."

I thought I had lucked out when the hostess seated me at my favorite table near a window all by myself. But not five minutes later, another resident joined me. The sequined busybody from the bingo game earlier. She just plopped herself right down into the seat opposite me. No invitation. Just sat herself down where she pleased. I couldn't even blame the hostess, who was busy breaking up a fight between two of the other female residents, both of whom wanted the one available seat at the table served by the only cute male waiter on staff.

"If you don't mind," I said, "I was saving the seat for someone else."

I wasn't, of course, but she didn't need to know that.

"I have something very important to tell you," she said, paying no mind to my gesturing at her to vacate the seat.

"Let me guess. You won another bingo."

"No, of course not," she snapped. "That was just part of my act. You know, the senile old lady who can barely remember to dress herself each morning before leaving her room."

Now she had my attention.

"You see, dear," she continued, "when everyone thinks you're crazy and can't remember a damn thing, they're much more willing to say things in front of you that they would otherwise keep to themselves. You'd be surprised at how much you can learn from people who speak freely in your presence when they believe you either can't understand or won't remember what you've overheard."

I had to admit, she put on a pretty good show. She could do crazy better than anyone else I'd seen in a long time.

"So that explains the sequined outfits. A costume of sorts to throw off any suspicion that you might, indeed, be lucid?" I asked.

"No, I just like to sparkle. Makes every day a little brighter, don't you think? Do you have a problem with that?"

I told her I didn't.

"I don't think we've been formally introduced," she continued. "I'm Cheshire, Cheshire Lively."

Was she serious?

"But everyone calls me Chessy."

"Millie Holt," I responded. "Pleasure to meet you. So, Chessy, how did you end up at Springtime Pastures? You seem pretty ambulatory to me, and if you're as lucid as you claim to be, what are you doing here?"

"It's a story as old as time. Girl meets boy. Girl marries boy. Girl and boy have a child. Girl and boy plan to grow old together. Boy dies from a long and debilitating illness. Girl uses every bit of their life savings taking care of boy before he dies. Girl then moves in with child. Girl becomes unhappy living with child because she's not getting the attention she deserves. Girl then devises a plan to convince said child to foot the bill for a permanent residency in a retirement village where there would be more activities and stimulation. Girl accomplishes this by pretending to have a touch of dementia but not enough to require a memory care facility. Child researches Springtime Pastures and dumps girl into the cheapest housing here that still qualifies her for the skilled nursing facility when it becomes necessary. How did you end up here?"

I figured I had nothing to lose, so I told her, including the part about the non-licensed electrician I had hired to support my herbal supplement side hustle. She was impressed and said I seemed like her kind of people. She asked me if I had ever considered wearing sequined outfits on a regular basis, to which I said no, though not before she had offered to lend me some of hers. Never mind the fact that she was easily in her eighties and about six inches shorter than I was. Maybe she wasn't quite as lucid as she claimed to be.

Our server came by and took our dinner orders, as I had reluctantly allowed Chessy to continue occupying the seat opposite me. None of the options on tonight's menu sounded particularly appealing to me, so I had asked for a steak but was told they didn't stock steaks of any kind on the premises. I wasn't a steak eater anyway, so it didn't matter. I was more interested in seeing the reaction on the server's face when I asked for one. I could tell that I wasn't the first resident ever to have made such a request, though. I was pretty sure that, for most of the residents in B-Block, steak was strictly restricted from their diets for medical reasons. I ended up ordering a bland chicken dish.

Chessy, on the other hand, put in a special request for a pimento cheese sandwich on white bread. If you're not familiar with pimento cheese, it really is a southern delicacy. Shredded Cheddar and Jack cheeses or perhaps Colby Jack instead, pimentos, and a ton of mayonnaise. Oh, and if you're feeling really adventurous, throw in some green olives, too.

Springtime Pastures had its own take on the recipe, though, substituting the required ingredients for their low- or no-fat versions. I tried it once and, well, I accidentally ate a shoelace once that tasted better than that crap. Granted I was on a psychedelic trip at the time, but still, my taste buds were fully intact. I gave Chessy a warning look as she placed her order, but she seemed unfazed. She may have dressed to sparkle, but apparently, she didn't give a damn about the taste of her food.

"All right," I said as I leaned over the table, "you said you had something you needed to tell me. Go ahead; I'm all ears."

"Yes. Well, you'll never guess what I overheard when I was loitering outside Julie's office after the bingo game, pretending I couldn't find my way back to my room."

"I imagine you probably heard more crying. Julie's well of tears seems to have no bottom as far as I could tell," I laughed.

"No. Well, maybe a little. But she was talking to someone on the phone. It took me awhile to figure out who she was speaking with. But I eventually did."

"And?" I asked, getting a little impatient.

"Well, I could only hear one side of the conversation, but she addressed the man on the other end of the call as 'Mr. Finch.'"

That gave me pause. Scott's last name was Finch. But Julie had explicitly told me that she had never met his parents. I supposed she could have looked them up and wanted to call them to break the bad news. I also wasn't sure I understood why Chessy here would want me to know about this call. Had she known about Scott and Julie's little romance before today?

"What else did you hear?" I asked, prodding her along ever so gently.

"She was telling Mr. Finch that she was pregnant with Scott's child."

Julie didn't have much tact. That was for sure. Who tells a father that his son passed away unexpectedly and then informs said father in the same conversation that he's going to be a grandfather? That said, I was still waiting for Chessy to tell me something I really needed to know, and I was on my last nerve by this point in time.

But then a thought started to percolate, and I asked Chessy to assess the tone of Julie's voice as she was relaying the news of her pregnancy to Mr. Finch. Was she telling him simply to let him know? Or did she want something from him? Financial support, perhaps? Maybe Scott's parents were devoutly religious, and the idea of Scott having a child out of wedlock was completely unacceptable to them. And if Julie knew that, she could have been naming her terms to keep quiet about the baby. Julie herself came from a devoutly religious background. Perhaps she and Scott had bonded over their shared experiences.

"Well, she tried at first to speak in a very sensitive tone. Like she knew she had to tell him something he wasn't going to like. She tried to put some genuine feeling in her voice, you know, consoling the grieving father with the news that his son will live on in his grandchild."

Okay, so perhaps there was no ulterior motive, I thought. Too early to tell for sure, though.

"Julie then offered to stay in touch with Scott's parents, but I couldn't get a read on how Mr. Finch reacted to that. What I do know is that he must have asked her about how Scott had died because the next thing I knew, Julie had mentioned you by name as the woman who found his body. There was another pause, and then Julie replied that she didn't think you had anything to do with it. Then another pause. And finally, Julie said, 'Well, I suppose she could have.'"

"Wait a minute," I said, barely able to catch my breath, "are you saying she said I might have had something to do with Scott's death?"

"That's what it sounded like to me," Chessy replied. "I figured you'd want to know."

What was it with people today accusing me of murder? Do I look like a murderer? Do I sound like a murderer? Do I unknowingly give off some sort of murderer vibe? As if reading my mind, she reassured me that I didn't have anything to worry about.

"You see," she continued, "I was a forensic psychologist before my husband's illness forced me into retirement. I'm pretty good at sizing up people, what they're capable of and what they aren't."

A former forensic psychologist named Cheshire Lively who now dresses in head-to-toe sequins every day. Whoever would have thought?

"What's your assessment of Julie?" I asked. "Is she capable of murder? Does she have it in herself to off a former lover who scorned her? I'm not saying that's what happened, but it's certainly possible."

"No, I don't think so," Chessy responded. "Julie has her own issues, but murder isn't one of them. Her weakness is that she places her own self-worth in the hands of those she loves. It's why she's never been able to hold onto a relationship for more than six months. I've gotten to know her pretty well during my stay here."

"Oh, I think she's got a couple of other big weaknesses myself, but if this is her big one, then do you think it's possible that Scott had recently broken up with Julie? Or maybe the other way around? Maybe she was already mourning the loss of the relationship before Scott passed away this morning."

Chessy didn't agree with this assessment, stating that she was pretty sure Julie and Scott were still an item before his untimely death, based on how Julie was speaking with Scott's father on the phone. I couldn't argue with that, given how upset Julie was when I broke the news to her earlier in the day. I then asked Chessy if there was anything else she was able to glean from the conversation she had overheard.

"Now, that you mention it, yes," she said. "She asked Mr. Finch if they would be coming down from Connecticut to deal with everything here. Like figuring out where Scott's final resting place would be and beginning the process of establishing Scott's estate. Given that Scott was still fairly young, he probably didn't have a will. But there was one part of the exchange that caught me off guard. Julie asked Mr. Finch if he thought they might seek to have an autopsy done, and from her reaction a few seconds later, I'm pretty sure Mr. Finch had said no. Seemed a little fishy to me. If my son had suddenly passed away, I'd want to know how and why."

Me too, I thought. *Me too.*

7

I woke up the next morning to my cell phone ringing. It was Anna Lee wanting to know if I'd had a chance to speak with Julie yet about whether Scott had any pre-existing health conditions and whether she had a way to get into his domicile. I tell you, for a woman who had made it perfectly clear on numerous occasions that I was beneath her social status, she certainly was interested in me now. I told her I'd try to find Julie sometime today, and I meant it too. I had to do what I could to mitigate whatever damage she had done by telling Scott's father that I possibly could have had something to do with his son's death.

After taking a shower and dressing in a pair of jean shorts and a gray T-shirt, I headed down to the dining room for some breakfast. It had taken me awhile to get the hang of how to correctly have breakfast in a retirement home setting. If you want actual eggs and not the frozen crap that simply gets reheated, you have to ask for them. If you want cheese on your eggs, you have to specify that you want real shredded cheese and not the awful slices of processed sandwich cheese that they will otherwise use. And finally, if you want real bacon, you practically have to get on your hands and knees and beg for the good stuff. They don't like the residents to get on their hands and knees because most of the residents can't get back up! So threatening to do so will usually get you the real thing.

What I hadn't anticipated, on this otherwise ordinary morning, was that I would find myself seated at a table with Rebecca, Lanie, and Anna Lee. The dining room in B-Block was technically open to all residents of Springtime Pastures; those who didn't live in the prison had to pay to eat here, though. And they had to pay in cash, which probably meant that Lanie was treating the other women to breakfast this morning, since she was the most likely of the three to still carry large sums of cash on her person at all times. I wasn't sure whether it was because she was afraid to use a credit card, being the paranoid basket case that she really was, or because she wanted to show off her wealth, but I was betting on the latter.

"All right," I said as I settled into my seat. "What the hell is going on?"

"Well, dear, we wanted to stop in to see you and continue our little conversation from yesterday," Anna Lee said. "The three of us had a little conference call last night, and we all agreed that we weren't sure how seriously you were taking the possibility that our beloved Scotty's death wasn't from natural causes. You seemed reluctant to proceed as we all had agreed, asking Julie or whatever her name was if she could get us into Scotty's home. We, well, we all felt that we should pay you a visit to make sure you're going to follow through on your word. It pains me to say that you weren't very convincing on the phone earlier. There was no urgency in your voice, dear."

"I still say she did it," Lanie whispered into Anna Lee's ear loudly enough for all of us to hear.

I was about to start in on Lanie when, out of the corner of my eye, I caught Chessy staring at us. I was tempted to bring her over here so she could give me her expert opinion on these ladies at a later point in time, but I didn't want to blow her cover. All I could do was hope that she could make her observations from afar. She happened to be wearing a blue-sequined number today, with shiny silver flats and a handbag to match. Her child must pay a small fortune in dry-cleaning bills every month.

"Listen," I said as a waiter came over to our table to take our breakfast orders, "I agreed to speak with Julie today, and I will. I'm a woman of my word. Now, tell this tattooed and pierced young man here what you want to eat. We'll get back to the business at hand afterward."

They all looked up at him with a bit of trepidation. Sure, he was a little rough on the eyes, but I had always considered it a part of his charm. There was something endearing about the particular way he spiked up his jet-black hair. Like he's strutting his feathers or something. I think he purposely overdoes it with the hair to spite his old man, who happens to be one of the administrators here at Springtime Pastures. I don't know all the details, but basically, his father forces him to work here to help pay off some debts our waiter acquired on account of an unfortunate incident involving a girl he was dating. She opened up a bunch of credit cards in his name and then split once she maxed them all out.

After a little prodding from me, the ladies all ordered variations of eggs, meat, and toast. I thought about clueing them in beforehand on how to order a good meal here in B-Block, but I decided to have a little fun with them and watch their expressions sour as their food arrived and they realized that they weren't exactly getting a gourmet meal. As for me, I ordered a bowl of cereal and a banana. It's the one thing they can't seem to screw up here, no matter how hard they try.

"Now, as I said, I will talk to Julie today," I reiterated. "Satisfied?"

"No," Rebecca answered, "we're coming with you. We're going to stick to you like glue for the rest of the day."

"But you don't even know Julie. You didn't even know she existed until I mentioned her name. Which is curious," I said as I fixed my gaze on Anna Lee, "given your alleged friendship with Scott outside our water aerobics class. You'd think he would have said *something* about Julie to you."

"I, um, well," Anna Lee sputtered, "he didn't mention her by name."

"Right, I'm betting he didn't mention her at all. Which leads me to another point. There's a whole lot about Scott's life that we don't know. We could be in for the shock of our lives if we do go snooping around his home. We could find all sorts of things that might upset the more delicate among us," I said as I pivoted my gaze toward Lanie.

"Like what?" Lanie demanded to know.

"Well, we might discover he's a Democrat," I laughed, knowing that Lanie was about as ruby-red Republican as you can get.

You'd be surprised what you can learn about a person when you share a pool with them a couple of mornings a week. Especially during an election season. Lanie actually put up GOP signs in her front yard, which got her in trouble for violating community standards regarding external décor. Anna Lee was an old-school Southern Democrat who voted more Republican these days but not always. Rebecca, on the other hand, was a dyed-in-the-wool yellow dog Democrat.

As for myself, I couldn't give two shits about either party. Neither one had done much to legalize my herbal supplement side hustle and favorite pastime. So no, I was more of an anti-political, anti-establishment type. Neither party had ever done much for me, so I was much more inclined to vote third party or not at all. Boy did I get an earful from all sides on that one during this last go around. They all had various ways of telling me that I was wasting my vote. I didn't care.

"Not funny!" Lanie responded. "And not possible. I have it on good authority that Scotty was a good God-fearing Republican."

Rebecca rolled her eyes.

"Lanie," I said, "I doubt that you have any better idea what political party he belonged to than the rest of us, and it doesn't even matter in the end. Besides, I was only joking. What I was trying to do was make a point that we might learn some things about Scott that could tarnish our opinions of him. We have no idea what we'll find. Better to be prepared going into this than not."

"I couldn't have said it better myself," Anna Lee added. "Yes, it's true: we all probably have our assumptions about how Scotty lived his life. And yes, some of us here might be a little more informed than others. But I've always felt that he was holding back from me a bit. Even during our many late-night private meetings."

It was my turn to roll my eyes. She just couldn't help herself. I know that "regaling" present company with colorful stories is a southern tradition and all, or at least that's how the movies portray us southerners, but why does she have to cross the line between exaggeration and outright lies?

"Anna Lee," Rebecca said, "you've had about as many of these late-night interludes as I've got fingers outstretched on my hand right now."

She was holding only one finger up, and I'm sure you can guess which one it happened to be. Anna Lee recoiled, and Lanie let out a little chirp of surprise. I sighed. This was going to be a long day for me if I had to spend it with these three women. Thankfully, our food arrived a moment later, which broke the tension a bit, at least until they realized that what they each had received on their plates was a mere imitation of what they had actually ordered.

"How do you eat this food day in and day out?" Rebecca asked me as she glanced mournfully at the reheated egg patty on her plate.

"Oh, you learn what's safe and what's not. Little tricks of the trade here and there. Cereal is usually a safe bet," I said as I pointed to my own bowl.

Lanie not so subtly implied that I should have given them all some pointers on what not to order. I, in response, not so subtly implied that they should have given me some warning before showing up en masse in my dining room with the intention of lighting a fire under my keister.

Anyway, we ate the remainder of our meals in silence, or rather, I polished my banana and bowl of cereal off while the others picked at their food, only eating enough to sustain their own overprivileged lives until lunchtime. I was pretty sure there would be no repeat performance of the three of them showing up uninvited to share a meal with me here in B-Block. And that suited me just fine.

After Lanie paid the bill for the three of them, we left the dining room in search of Julie. I knew she wasn't likely to be in her office at this hour, since she was habitually late to work, but I figured we'd start there. No luck. I then took them to the social room where I helped run the bingo game yesterday, figuring if she was on the premises and not in her office, then this is where she would be. Nope. I then led us all to the small library, where she sometimes led a story hour, but she wasn't there either.

I was about to give up when I thought of one other place she might be. The on-site salon. And sure enough, there she was, pilfering supplies as I had suspected. I had caught her in the act once before, though she hadn't seen me. What a woman her age needed with ammonium thioglycolate was beyond me, but well, I kept her little secret as an insurance policy of sorts. I had the goods on her, and I was prepared to deploy them if she should ever find my contraband booze and truly make a move to get me kicked out of here.

But now I was stuck. I wasn't the only one witnessing this latest theft. Lanie, Rebecca, and Anna Lee were with me! So, I did what anyone would do in such a circumstance. I yelled "JULIE" at the top of my lungs. She just about hit the ceiling in fright. Bingo!

"Oh, hi," she said as she attempted to pull herself together and hide the bottle of shampoo she was undoubtedly about to stuff into her oversized handbag. "Didn't see you standing there, Millie. Oh, and look! You have friends with you!"

"We are not her friends," Lanie snapped. "We're acquainted with Millie. Nothing more."

"But we do have a shared purpose now," Anna Lee added.

I introduced everyone to Julie and then explained why we were here and what we wanted to know from her. She said Scott hadn't had any pre-existing health conditions that she knew of, which was a relief to some of us and yet very unsettling to me. On one hand, such a health condition would have at least lessened the possibility in our minds that Scott's death was the result of foul play. On the other hand, I think I can speak for all of us in saying that it would have saddened us greatly to know that such a young man died of natural causes.

We then moved on to the subject of Scott's domicile, whether she knew where he lived and if so, did she have a way to gain access. She was a little cagey at first, initially denying that she had ever set foot inside his place. All it took was one stern look from Rebecca, and she folded like a cheap tent. She admitted to sleeping over at his place many, many times and said that, while she didn't have her own key, she was pretty sure she knew where Scott had hidden a spare. I asked her for Scott's address and the approximate location of said spare key. She demurred.

"Julie," Anna Lee said, "we really do need to, um, take a look around Scotty's place before the police do. We all believe that his death wasn't some sort of accident, and we'd like to poke around a bit to see if we can start figuring out what might have actually happened. You do want to know if anyone was involved in Scotty's death, don't you? If there was a perpetrator of sorts, don't you believe it would be best for him to be found out and put away before you give birth to Scotty's child? For all you know, the perpetrator could have some sort of vendetta against Scotty's entire family, including any illegitimate offspring."

Illegitimate offspring? Did Anna Lee really just say that? I knew she was old-school and all, but still. I thought she'd have a little more tact than that. Julie looked at her, seeming not to comprehend what she had just said. So, I explained it to her in terms I knew she would understand, and finally, the light bulb turned on.

"Will you help us?" Lanie asked, unsure what else she could do to move the situation along.

Julie looked me in the eye, trying to determine how serious I was about being a part of this whole plan. When I didn't blink, she agreed. Damn, I'm good.

"But I'm coming with you all," she added. "You elderly ladies need supervision. Meet me out front at 6:30 p.m. We'll go from there."

"One more thing," I said as I looked directly at Julie, "just so everyone is clear on this. I did not kill Scott. Nor did I have anything to do with his death."

8

We arrived at Scott's place of residence, all five of us, right as the sun was setting. Julie had driven us in her big black SUV, since we couldn't have all comfortably fit into any of our other cars. I had to say I was impressed by the appearance of Scott's house. It was a cute little bungalow with a wide front porch holding a pair of rocking chairs. The paint color was somewhere between taupe and brown, and the trim was done in a very appealing cream color. You don't often come across a bachelor's house that looks so well put together and maintained, unless, of course, the bachelor has a lot of money and can afford to pay others to do all the work.

After getting out of the SUV, we followed Julie around to the back of the house and up onto the rear deck, which was adorned with pots full of vegetables. I had no idea Scott had such a green thumb. Julie lifted up the side of a pot containing a cucumber plant and retrieved what appeared to be a spare key to the house. She then gave us all one last look, as if she were asking us if we were sure we really wanted to proceed inward. When none of us flinched, she acquiesced, inserted the key into the lock, and turned it to open the door.

Then all chaos ensued. We were greeted by a blisteringly loud alarm system that was angrily screeching, "Intruder Alert! Intruder Alert!" Anna Lee tried to steady herself against the side of the house but failed and slumped onto the deck. Lanie ran back down the steps and toward the SUV like her life depended on it. Rebecca was doing her best to cover her ears but remained firmly planted in place otherwise, while Julie and I stepped inside in search of the alarm panel. I was praying that Julie knew the code to shut the damn thing off.

We eventually did find the panel, which was oddly located in the master bedroom, and Julie managed to disarm it, though she covered the panel with one hand while she punched in the code with the other so I couldn't see. I wanted to ask her what difference it made now whether I saw the code since Scott was dead but decided to err on the side of tact and dropped the issue. Fortunately, Julie was also under the impression that, while the house was armed, the alarm system wasn't actually monitored, so we weren't likely to see any police cars show up. She said Scott only used the alarm to deter would be burglars when he wasn't home. I thought we'd be lucky to find Anna Lee back on the deck still breathing. *Forget deterrent*, I thought, *and think more along the lines of instant death from cardiac arrest.*

I went back outside once Julie had the alarm system disarmed and bent over Anna Lee to see if there was still any life left in her aged body. She looked up at me in bewilderment and asked me how she had wound up in her current position. I left Rebecca to tend to her while I chased down Lanie, who looked like she was about to launch into some sort of hysterical orbit. She was pounding on the windows of the SUV, yelling at anyone who would listen to let her in. She was that scared. It took all the restraint I had not to slap her.

Instead, I gently placed my right hand on her right shoulder to alert her that I was there. She spun around so quickly that I thought she was going to lose her balance. I thought it would be such a shame if she fell flat on those fake knockers of hers and damaged them in the process. I'm not judging her for having them, mind you, but I am judging her for pretending they were real. Unless, of course, she was a cancer survivor and had gotten the implants as part of her reconstructive surgery. Then I could almost understand. Almost, but not quite. She wasn't worthy of any benefit of doubt on my part. Not after accusing me of killing poor Scott.

As Lanie realized she was now face to face with me, she dialed the hysterics down a bit and tried as best she could to get control of herself. It actually took her a moment to process the fact that the alarm had been turned off and that we weren't all going to be carted off by the police.

"I'm sorry," she said. "I don't know what came over me. I'm usually cool as a cucumber under pressure."

"Well, no, you're not, but it's nice that you think you are. Makes life easier if you're unable to see your own weaknesses, I suppose."

"And what is that supposed to mean?" she demanded to know.

"Oh, never mind," I responded, not wanting to start an argument with her. "Let's just get into the house and finish what we came here to do. Do you need to hold on to me for support?"

"No, thank you. I'm perfectly capable of managing on my own."

"Fine. Suit yourself," I said.

We walked back up the stairs to the deck and gave a helping hand to Rebecca, who was struggling to get Anna Lee back up into an erect position. Julie should have come back out to help, but when the rest of us finally entered the house together, we found Julie sobbing on a sofa, hugging a blanket close to her chest and burying her face in its fibers.

"It still smells like him," Julie said through the tears now streaming down her face.

I sat down on the couch and tried my best to comfort her, but it didn't work. The tears turned into a flood, and before I knew it, she was ugly crying. There was really no way to stop her now. She was going to have to go through it and hopefully come out the other side in a better state of mind. We had a mission to complete here, and since she knew the layout of Scott's house while the rest of us didn't, we needed her help.

Holding a still-sobbing Julie in my arms, I took a good look around the living room, trying to see if anything here might bring some sort of inspiration about where else to look or what to do next. The couch we were sitting on was made of a pretty high-end fabric, and the other pieces of furniture looked equally expensive. Very rich wood tones, and nothing made of particle board, as far as I could tell. There was a striking abstract painting on the far wall, at least five feet by five feet that looked somewhat like a butterfly. The entire room seemed to have been decorated around this one piece of art. As much as I would have liked to believe Scott did all this on his own, I had my doubts. But then again, did I ever truly know him?

I gently extricated myself from Julie's grasp after a few more moments had passed and walked around to the kitchen, hoping to find some inspiration in there. The décor was a bit austere for my tastes but stunning, nonetheless. White Shaker-style upper cabinets, a light-gray glass-tile backsplash, Carrara marble countertops and black lower cabinets. High-end stainless-steel appliances surrounded me from every angle, and a deep, inset stainless-steel sink and matching faucet completed the picture. Unfortunately, nothing seemed to be amiss, even after I peered into the refrigerator. Nothing but healthy foods portioned out into individual meals ready for Scott to take with him wherever he needed to be.

I was about to start rummaging through some of the cabinets before stopping in fright.

"Does anyone have any gloves on them?" I asked the rest of the group still seated in the living room.

"Why?" Lanie asked in response.

"Well, because it just occurred to me that, even though Scott's house isn't itself a crime scene, someone's bound to come sniffing around looking for clues, like we're doing right now. Based on the current state of things in here, I doubt the police have made an appearance yet, but don't you think they eventually will?"

"What are you getting at?" Anna Lee asked.

"What she's getting at," Rebecca interjected, "is that we don't want to leave any fingerprints behind. We don't want to leave any evidence for the police to find that would indicate that we were ever here."

The women all started riffling through their purses, hoping against hope that they'd magically find a pair of gloves that they knew didn't actually exist.

"Ugh," I said, and then used my shirt to open a couple of drawers until I found what I was looking for. Oven mitts. There were enough to go around, so I grabbed them all and brought them back into the living room.

"You can't be serious," Lanie said. "How are we going to sift through papers or whatever else we might find while wearing these?"

"As delicately and as ladylike as we can," Anna Lee answered. "Whatever we do must be done with the utmost care. Think about all those cotillion lessons we had as girls. Every action must be planned and executed with a purpose."

Rebecca informed us that cotillions weren't really a thing up North, and I had certainly never attended one myself. I doubted Lanie had either, and I was pretty certain Julie hadn't. From what I gathered, her family wouldn't have approved of her dancing with members of the opposite sex, ever.

"Am I the only one here who was taught how to be a lady? The only one here who was exposed to culture as a child?" Anna Lee asked, genuinely shocked and disheartened.

"No, Anna Lee," Rebecca replied. "You were merely shown a version of culture and society. We all come from different places with different cultural practices and expectations. I'm not saying any single one is superior to the others, but well, let's just say some are less equal than the rest."

Anna Lee was about to respond when I held my hand up to silence them both and to remind everyone present that we were on a mission here. We didn't have time to sit here and reenact the Civil War. We needed to move quickly. I suggested we split up into teams. I wanted Rebecca and Julie with me, as I thought they were the two most capable among us. And I figured Anna Lee and Lanie could do whatever it is they normally do when they're trying but failing to be helpful. Everyone grudgingly agreed to the plan, and I took Rebecca and Julie with me toward the back of the house where the bedrooms were located, leaving the other two to look for any clues they could find in the living areas.

I started to put on one of the oven mitts as we made our way back, but Rebecca stopped me.

"You're not going to need that," she said. "It's highly unlikely that any of us have our fingerprints registered in some federal crimes database, so even if the police discover our fingerprints here, they won't know who they belong to. And no one with any sense is going to believe that we had any involvement in Scott's death."

"Well, why didn't you say something before?" I asked.

"Because I wanted a good look at Lanie and Anna Lee trying their hardest to lift things up and peer into drawers, hampered by those oven mitts. Gotta take your moments of humor where you can find them!"

Julie chastised Rebecca for being so mean spirited, but I started laughing. The mental picture Rebecca had painted was quite humorous, and I had trouble regaining my composure. If I ever do take Lanie out in a canoe and then capsize the vessel, I'll have to make sure to tie oven mitts to her hands first. As if my little fantasy couldn't get any better!

We started our search in the master bedroom, where Julie showed us around as if we couldn't find our own way around a bedroom to save our lives. There was a king-size four-poster bed set against the far wall, with a nightstand and lamp on each side. A chest of drawers was tucked away in a corner, and what was most likely a little reading nook with a lime-green armchair, a cherrywood end table, and a Tiffany lamp was set up in the corner closest to us. Again, I had this overwhelming feeling that Scott couldn't possibly have put this room together on his own.

Rebecca started rummaging through the nightstand drawers while Julie and I went into the bathroom. I was searching for a medicine cabinet to see if maybe we'd find some clues in there. Like, could someone have switched out his medications without him knowing? Once I located it, I opened the door and took a look at its contents. He kept some of his toiletries in there, but not much in the way of medicine. There was prescription for what I thought was a cholesterol medication and another one that I've used myself for allergies. But that was about it.

I began to close the door to the medicine cabinet, but instead, I grabbed the two pill bottles and shoved them into my pocketbook. Julie asked me why I had taken them, but I decided against telling her the truth. If she was going to suggest to Scott's father that I possibly could have had something to do with his son's death, I needed to keep her at arm's length. I didn't completely trust her, and since she pretty much already fulfilled her usefulness here by getting us inside the house, I didn't see the need to cooperate with her. When she pressed me again, I told her I took the exact same prescriptions and had run out of both of them this very morning. She bought it hook, line, and sinker. My plan, however, was to see if I could send them off to a lab to be tested. You know, to make sure someone hadn't messed with his medications.

We left the bathroom and rejoined Rebecca in the bedroom where she was still sifting through the various papers and other items that she had retrieved from the nightstand drawers. I started to tell her that she should have given more care to what she was doing, so she'd be able to remember to put everything back exactly as she found it. But did it really matter? I mean, the only person who was going to know that anything was out of place was Scott, and he was dead.

"Have you found anything of interest?" I asked her.

"Not yet, lots to go through. Sit down and help me with this. The more sets of eyes we have, the better," she responded.

I took a seat next to her on the bed, and she handed me a handful of papers to start digging through. Julie took a seat on my other side, but I suggested to her that she go check on Lanie and Anna Lee. She didn't want to go, but I told her that I was concerned for Anna Lee's health after the incident with the alarm and would feel better if a health professional would go and assess Anna Lee's current condition. Julie reminded me that she was an activities director and not a nurse, to which I responded that if she was going to dress like a nurse, she might as well act like a nurse.

9

With Julie out of the way, Rebecca and I dug into the piles of papers and other items she had removed from the nightstands. Given Scott's youthful age, I was surprised to find so much paper in the first place. My daughter and her husband pretty much ran their whole lives electronically, and Scott was several years younger than they were, so why I was looking at bills, bank statements, letters, photos, and other printed materials I couldn't quite explain. But it certainly beat trying to figure out the password to his computer for the time being, not that we had laid eyes on said computer yet. It was probably in one of the other bedrooms he may have set up as some sort of home office. And if we weren't easily able to locate his computer in the end, I was sure Julie would know where it was.

We started looking through the letters together, figuring it would be better for us both to do so in case one of us missed something, some pertinent detail that might actually matter in the grand scheme of things. Hopefully the other would catch it. Some of the letters were from women who turned out to be ex-girlfriends of his, or rather I should say they were printouts of emails from them. These were mostly breakup letters. I couldn't believe these women hadn't given Scott the courtesy of breaking up with him to his face or even over the phone. No, they did it via email. *Cowards,* I thought. I mean, what's the point in living if you're going to live your life in fear of personal conflict? Hell, half the fun in living is telling people off to their faces!

Why would Scott have kept these letters, and could any of these ex-girlfriends have had something to do with Scott's death? Some of the women were pretty upset, going on and on about how much they loved him but weren't feeling the same intensity of love in return. One of them even talked about how the sex life had completely ceased to exist several months into the relationship. Hell hath no fury like a woman who wants some but isn't getting any. Or so I've been told. I hadn't had that problem myself, at least not until I moved into Springtime Pastures six months ago where the attractive, available men were few and far between.

I wanted to take these breakup letters with us, but Rebecca suggested that she use her phone to take pictures of them instead, explaining that she didn't think we'd want to impede any official police investigation by confiscating evidence. And we certainly didn't want the police to find out that we had been here and taken them. I couldn't argue with that, especially since I was a reluctant participant in this whole charade to begin with. She took the breakup letters back over to the nightstand, took pictures of them one by one and then placed them back into the top drawer.

We then sifted through some more letters, some from old friends, some from his swimming buddies from the Olympics and other various competitions. Nothing in these letters seemed out of the ordinary to either of us, mostly letters checking in with Scott over the last couple of years to see how he was getting along post-injury. Rebecca asked me if I thought we should take pictures of these letters, as well, like I was some sort of expert on investigating murders or something. I told her I didn't think there was much value in these, and if we were wrong, surely the police would determine otherwise.

Next, we went through the pile of bills, mostly utility bills, cable bills, and cell phone bills. He had collected and kept each bill from each provider going back several years. I was starting to think maybe he was a hoarder of some sort, maybe in the early stages of the illness. Or maybe he was an obsessive compulsive, and I simply never knew. Rebecca pointed out that these bills were all in black and white, meaning they were copies and not the originals. Each bill had a hand-written "paid" somewhere near the bottom. Very beautiful handwriting, but I wondered if it was his. I didn't have anything else to compare the handwriting to at the moment, though. I asked Rebecca to take pictures of some of the bills in case there was something that we were overlooking in the heat of the moment.

What didn't escape my notice was that there were no mortgage statements or rent bills. I asked Rebecca if she thought that perhaps Scott owned the house outright, but she looked doubtful. I mean, sure, it was possible. Maybe he came from money. But if he didn't, I couldn't see how he could have afforded to buy a house outright at his age and with his known work history. Seemed a little too far-fetched to both of us.

Fortunately, we didn't have to wonder for long. The next pile of papers contained a ton of bank statements. Even I didn't receive printed bank statements anymore, but here they were, and they weren't copies. They were originals with a little blue image in the shape of North Carolina and the words State Employees Credit Union. How he managed to get an account there, I didn't know since he wasn't a state employee and definitely didn't live with a state employee. Maybe one of his ex-girlfriends was a state employee? We'd have to investigate that later.

We split up the bank statements between us and began pouring over them, looking for any irregularities. And sure enough, we both started seeing a pattern of deposits into Scott's account from another account. At first, we weren't sure if maybe he was transferring money from one account to another, but we quickly realized that he only had one account listed at the top of the summary page for each statement. No, these deposits were coming from someone else's account, though we didn't know whose. There was no identifying information other than the last four digits of the account number from which these transfers were being made.

Judging by the beginning and ending balances on each statement and by the amounts of these recurring transfers, it looked like these transfers were enough to cover all of his bills and then some. Actually, quite a lot of money. Combining our two separate piles of statements into one, we took another look at them in chronological order and tracked the increasing balances over time. It looked like his paychecks from Springtime Pastures weren't even being used to cover any of his daily living expenses, like food and gas. Someone was supporting him financially and pretty generously so. Rebecca took pictures of the last six months' worth of statements and then returned them to the nightstand once we were sure we hadn't missed anything else that we wanted to document.

Moving on to the photos we found, and there were plenty, I wished I could say they were of some value to our little amateur investigation, but for the most part they weren't. At least Scott had organized the majority of them into a photo album, yet another skill I was surprised he had, given his youthful age. Prior to this evening, I would have been surprised if anyone under forty these days would know what to do with a photo album if it up and bit them on the ass. But Scott had organized his photos in chronological order. Very impressive.

We skimmed through his childhood pretty quickly, noting his parents and siblings out of curiosity's sake and snapping a couple of pictures with Rebecca's phone. We made our way through his high school years with little to note of other than his swimming pictures; in every one of them he was wearing a Speedo. He was too young in those photos, though. Needed to grow a bit more, if you get my drift. When we did finally reach the photos from his professional swimming career, in which he was also wearing Speedos, I made Rebecca take pictures of those. No way was I walking away from this evening without a party favor! Do you think it would be in poor taste to have one of these photos blown up to poster size?

Nearing the end of the album, we discovered a couple of photos that weren't fastened to the pages but were stuck in there instead. Three photos to be exact. One was of Scott and a very attractive woman, both smiling and holding up wine glasses. They were decked out, too, so I figured this was probably taken at a wedding reception. I flipped the photo over to see if Scott had written any names on the back, but he hadn't. I had wondered if perhaps this was one of the exes who had broken up with him over email. I always like to put a face to the name when possible. The second photo was of Scott and another woman, less attractive than the first, but still cute. They must have been hiking somewhere in this one.

The third photo was the only one that provided any real interest. Scott was sitting at a table in what looked like a dimly lit restaurant, and he was seated opposite a man. The man wasn't his father, and I didn't recognize the face as belonging to any of the other men we had seen throughout the album. But there was something about this man, a familiarity. Like I had seen him somewhere before. I couldn't figure out where, though. I asked Rebecca if she knew who this man was, but she said she didn't. He was handsome, dressed in a suit, probably in his mid-forties, graying hair around his temples, and a pair of metal-framed glasses. I decided to take the photo with us, figuring it wouldn't do any harm to ruminate on who this man was a bit further and that no one would miss it. Rebecca didn't object.

All we had left to do was go through the physical objects that Rebecca had retrieved. A flashlight. Some batteries. A very expensive-looking pen. A notebook, which turned out to be empty, though it looked like a couple of pages had been torn out of it. A couple of tubes of lip balm. A gold watch. Ear plugs. A magnifying glass. Just your typical nightstand-storage items. We shoved everything back into the drawers and then made our way to the walk-in closet.

The closet itself was pretty ordinary, but it didn't take long to appreciate the thought Scott had put into how he organized his clothing. The shirts, both long- and short-sleeve, were arranged according to color. I was a little surprised at how many dress shirts he had, not understanding why a man of his vocation would need so many button-down shirts. He also had a number of suits, also arranged by color. Everything from a casual tan to a funeral-appropriate black. He also had a shoe rack with no less than ten pairs of dress shoes, several pairs of loafers and several lace-ups in black and various shades of brown.

I had turned around to leave the closet, figuring there was nothing in here worth investigating further, when Rebecca blocked my way.

"Check the pockets," she commanded.

I asked her why, but I realized what she was getting at as the words were leaving my mouth, so I turned around and started rummaging through the pockets of the suit jackets and pants. I was pretty sure Scott washed most of his clothes after a single wearing, but suits were different. They had to be dry-cleaned, which meant that Scott may have tried to get more than one wearing out of a suit before taking it to the cleaners. This was particularly true for a man living on a budget, though after looking at his bank statements a moment ago, I wasn't so sure that rationale applied to Scott. Still, even if he had some sort of benefactor who was supporting him, I was betting he was still reasonably frugal where he could be. He wasn't stupid, and I'm sure it wasn't lost on him that his benefactor could disappear at any moment, leaving him on very thin financial ice.

Most of the pockets were empty. It wasn't until we dug through the last suit, a black three-button style, that we found a crumpled-up piece of paper. We took the piece of paper back into the bedroom and over to one of the nightstands where we attempted to flatten it out. What we saw when we finally managed to do so was the name "Cardinal" and then a phone number below it. Rebecca was confused, and I had to admit I wasn't far behind her. We couldn't figure out who this name could have possibly belonged to. A person? A business? An organization? We were lost, but we decided to hold on to the piece of paper anyway. The police weren't going to miss it, we thought.

We quickly checked the other two bedrooms, but save for some furniture, there wasn't much to investigate. Both were set up as guest bedrooms and looked like they hadn't been used in years. The closets were bare, and the few drawers we found were empty. Well, at least Scott's parents weren't going to have to go through a mountain of his personal belongings when they sold the house. Curiously, though, we never did come across that pair of Speedos I bought him. I wondered where they ended up. I certainly hoped he hadn't thrown them away. I was a woman on a fixed income, and I wouldn't have taken kindly to having found out that my gift went straight into the garbage bin.

Making our way back into the living areas, we found Anna Lee and Lanie on one of the sofas and Julie in the armchair. I asked them if they had had any luck finding anything we needed to know about, but they hadn't. They had pretty much sat there the whole time we were in the bedrooms. Anna Lee claimed her heart hadn't yet recovered from the shock of that alarm system, and Lanie kept going on and on about how we were all going to get caught and end up in the slammer. Julie had decided it was best for her to stay near the two of them in case either ended up having an actual medical emergency.

Anna Lee asked if we had found any leads, and I said that we had but that perhaps we could meet sometime over the next day or two to discuss. Both she and Lanie seemed amenable to that, mostly because they were either too tired or too exhausted or too traumatized or any combination thereof to argue.

"Julie," I said as I turned in her direction, "one thing we haven't come across yet is a computer. A laptop, perhaps. Any idea where Scott might have kept one?"

She nodded and rose from her chair to go into the kitchen where she then opened one of the drawers in the bank of cabinets on the far wall. She retrieved a shiny silver laptop. I suggested that she also retrieve the charging cord, which she did. I opened the laptop on the kitchen countertop, hoping that it wasn't password protected, but no luck.

"Do you, by any chance, know what Scott's password is?" I asked Julie.

She shook her head, and my hopes sank.

10

I got a call next morning from Lanie asking me if I had figured out the password to Scott's laptop yet. When I told her I hadn't, she was "awfully disappointed." I told her it was unreasonable to expect that I would somehow magically come across the right combination of letters, numbers, and possibly special characters to gain access. She said she felt I wasn't trying hard enough and that a woman with as much character as I had should have been able to figure it out. And by "character," she meant crazy.

Rather than actually tell Lanie that I had a plan, which I did, I decided to have a little fun with her and tell her that I had a little tryst with a gentleman caller when I got home last night and that I had forgotten to remove the laptop from my bed before our bodies fell on top of it. She said she didn't believe me, which I took to mean she didn't think I was attractive enough to land any of the few eligible men left in this hen house. I responded that, unlike her hilarious attempts at seducing men by performing CPR on them when they didn't actually need it, I was actually having sex and plenty of it. She called me uncouth. I called her delusional. I told her I would be in touch once I figured out if the laptop was salvageable after the multiple dents my sex partner and I put into the thing, and then I ended the conversation.

I then got a call from Anna Lee a few minutes later, telling me not to worry about Lanie and that she'd have a little chat with her about her attitude toward me. Apparently, Lanie had already called her to complain about me. I told Anna Lee that I would appreciate that, and that if she couldn't get Lanie under control, they all could just count me out of this investigation going forward. Anna Lee promised to invite me over for another one of her tea socials to express her gratitude. I wanted to tell her I wasn't interested in any more gatherings at her place, but since she was trying to extend an olive branch on behalf of Lanie, I played along.

Like I said, I did have a plan for the laptop, which required me putting on clothes and going down to the dining room in search of a particular woman dressed in sequins from head to toe. I found said lady sitting alone at a table, talking to her spoon as if it were some sort of sentient being. She asked it if it enjoyed its oatmeal this morning and then added that, if it was really good, she would put some brown sugar in the next morning as a treat. I knew this was part of her act, of course, but that didn't stop me from whispering into her ear that I would love some brown sugar. She nearly fell out of her chair in shock but quickly recovered once I moved in front of her so she could see my face.

"Oh, it's you," Chessy said. "That was a mean trick, scaring an old woman who's half out of her mind as it is."

I took a seat and reminded her that she had already come clean to me about her act. I probably should have whispered that, but I didn't. The next thing I knew she was on her feet, ranting about how her silverware was giving her the silent treatment. She was just trying to cover for my lapse in judgment in broadcasting to all within earshot that she was indeed lucid.

"Sit back down," I whispered as I yanked on her sequined sleeve.

"Let go of me! You're going to rip my blouse."

I did as she commanded, and thankfully, she sat back down. However, every eye in the joint was now fixed squarely on us, and I had to figure out a way to divert those eyes elsewhere.

"Hey, look!" I said as I pointed toward the entrance. "There's Elvis! Elvis Presley! It's a miracle! He's alive!"

That did the trick. Several of the female residents even got out of their chairs and made their way toward the entrance and out into the hallway looking for him. Damn, I'm good.

"Very clever," Chessy remarked as she grudgingly nodded in approval. "You know how to read a room. Now, what do you want?"

"What, can't I simply pay a friendly visit to the neighborhood nut? Do I have to have some sort of ulterior motive?"

"You're forgetting who you're talking to, dear. I spent years reading people for money. You're on a mission. So, spill it. And do it quickly before those idiots who went looking for Elvis return. I would prefer to be back to my demented self before the dining room starts filling up again. Oh, and for the record, next time you host a bingo game here and I yell out that I have a bingo, would it kill you to simply say that I won, even if I didn't?"

"Wow, someone woke up on the wrong side of the bed this morning. You really shouldn't be wearing sequins today since your demeanor isn't exactly sparkling," I laughed.

"Yeah, well you try having a conversation with your offspring in which they inform you that you're being moved to the memory care ward when the next bed opens up."

"Oh, no," I said. "Can't you do something about this? Fight it somehow? Take a test to show you've still got your marbles—or at least enough of them to stay here in B-Block? Maybe I could help you in some way."

"Thank you, dear, but the problem is, I've played my part all too well. Who knew I could act so convincingly? You know, my late husband was into role playing. I wasn't, and I refused to play into his fantasies. But, well, I'm having regrets. I could have been a damn good naughty nurse. Or maybe a French maid. Or maybe something in leather."

"You still could! Find yourself one of the widowers here and give him the time of his life. You know, cross it off your bucket list and maybe his too."

"I like the way you think. Okay, so now that you have me in a more sparkly mood again, what is it that you wanted?"

"Well, first, I wanted to ask you what your take was on the three women that I had breakfast with yesterday morning. Your expert opinion. Like, if you had to create a psychological profile on them for one of your cases you were being asked to weigh in on."

"I wasn't really paying attention," Chessy responded, toying with me a little to see whether I would believe her.

"You can't fool me. Yes, you were. I caught you out of the corner of my eye looking very intensely at us, and since your vision and your hearing seem to be fully intact, they must have made some sort of impression on you."

"Yes, of course they did. How could they not?" she said. "The four of you are like points on a compass. Each point has its own unique direction, but together, you all form a useful instrument. Never forget that. And if the four of you are determined to figure out what happened to that poor pool instructor, you're going to have to rely on each other and play to each's strengths."

"So, what are our individual strengths as you see them?" I asked. "Because I'm only really seeing one of the three others as of being any use at all. The other two are all show and no go, at least in my experience so far."

"The short, stocky one, right? I can tell she means business, and she's not afraid to say what she thinks and then act accordingly. Judging by her mannerisms and her language skills, she's got some serious brain power behind her. She's analytical and can reason her way out of just about any problem or challenge she faces. She's the one in your little group who'll get you all out of a bind when you run up against a wall, like if the trail of clues suddenly goes cold. She'll figure out what to do next."

"What about the other two?" I pondered.

"The older of the two is a woman not to be messed with. Sure, she acts the part of a genteel aristocratic socialite, but underneath all that makeup and polish, she's a street fighter."

I had to laugh at this. The thought of dainty Anna Lee getting into a fight with anyone, risking even chipping a finely manicured nail, I didn't believe, and I told Chessy as much. She said I was wrong in my assessment, and that I would ignore her counsel at my peril, meaning that Anna Lee would do a whole lot more than bless my heart if I got on her bad side. But Chessy said that this was also a strength of Anna Lee's that could really come in handy depending on where the investigation led us.

I asked Chessy about Lanie next. She said Lanie was clearly a basket case, but that even she might prove useful in our investigative efforts, given that she presented an appearance of being well off financially. Chessy reminded me that money is power, and power opens doors that might otherwise remain locked to us. Money also affords one access to certain social circles that we might find of use, meaning that we might find ourselves at the mercy of powerful people with secrets they're unlikely to spill to anyone not in their social class. I supposed she had a point, and I conceded as much, since we had no leads at the moment. Lanie didn't have the kind of money that Anna Lee did, but she had enough that she was likely traveling in those upwardly mobile social circles.

After thanking Chessy for her insights, I moved on to my real purpose in coming down to the dining room to pick her brain. I asked her if she had any tips on how to crack open a laptop that we may or may not have found during a search that we may or may not have conducted on our own.

"Well, if you literally want to crack open a laptop, an ax would probably do the trick," she laughed. "But if you're looking to gain access to the laptop and are being stymied by a password that you can't figure out, you've got a couple of options."

"Go on. I'm listening," I urged.

"Option number one. Take the laptop to someone who knows how to hack into computers. There isn't a piece of electronic equipment out there that can't be hacked as long as the hacker knows what they're doing. Might cost you a pretty penny, though, so it depends on how much of your own money you want to put into this endeavor. Maybe one of the other ladies would be willing to pay?"

"Maybe. But I don't even know where I would begin to look for a reputable hacker. I don't want any of us to get taken for a ride. Maybe you have a connection you'd be willing to share?"

"Afraid not. I've been retired too long to still have any useful contacts for you in that area. Technology changes so quickly, and the tech people I knew when I was working weren't exactly spring chickens even back then."

"Well, damn," I said, feeling a bit defeated. "So, what's option two?"

"Option number two is to figure out the password. I know that sounds like an impossible task, but it really isn't. Most people mistakenly choose passwords that actually have some meaning to them. Some sort of significance. That's why so many people get hacked. Their passwords are simply too easy to guess."

"Any advice on where to start?" I asked, not looking forward to the task.

"How well did you know the pool instructor? What did you know about him? His birthday? His address? Any other important details from his life? Like certain dates or events or people?"

I told Chessy that I hadn't known Scott as well as I would have liked, and that while some of the other women claimed to have known him well, I was pretty sure they were exaggerating. It seemed like my best shot was to speak with Julie since she had actually had an intimate relationship with him. Certainly intimate enough to know where he kept his spare key. I just hoped that she'd be able to come up with some of the aforementioned details Chessy had suggested might help.

"Oh, and one more thing," I continued. "Any chance you'd be able to help me get some pills tested to see what they're actually made of?"

"I take it you found some pills at his house, along with his laptop?" she asked.

I grinned, maybe a little sheepishly.

"Bring them to me, and I'll take care of it," she said. "I know someone who'll test the pills without asking any questions."

I thanked her.

After eating a quick bowl of cereal while she reverted back into her dementia act, yet again conversing with her silverware, I returned to my cell to contemplate my next move. Julie hadn't been too happy when the four of us overruled her objection to taking Scott's laptop with us last night, so I was going to have to find a way to get on her good side once I saw her. And then, somehow, I was going to have to work Scott into the conversation, prodding her along when I wanted her to reveal specific details. Like details about his family, his favorite sports team, his first love, anything he might have used in creating that blasted password.

But then another problem arose. How was I going to remember all of these details? I wasn't sure I was ready to tell Julie why I was asking her these questions, so it would have been too obvious if I were to whip out a pad and pen to take notes. With a little more time, I could have figured out some way to wear an unobtrusive wire, one that she wouldn't notice. But, as it stood, I was going to have to find an excuse to take my phone out of my pocketbook and record the conversation on it without her realizing. Julie was a talker, and there was no way I'd be able to remember every little detail she might reveal that could be of some use. And that was assuming she'd even cooperate.

Come to think of it, I should have given the laptop to one of the other ladies for safekeeping, since Julie had the means and the motive to enter my cell on her own and confiscate it. The question was, *Would she*? There weren't many places in this cell of mine to hide the laptop where she couldn't find it. I supposed if she did, I could claim the laptop was mine and file a complaint, but if I did that, they'd likely ask me to enter in the correct password to prove that it was mine. And at least for the time being, I couldn't.

11

I went in search of Julie an hour later and found her in the library reading to some of the residents who can no longer read for themselves due to vision loss. Some of them received audiobooks in the mail from that free library service in Raleigh, but I think there's a community element involved here that audiobooks can't quite replicate. It's like coming together for a shared purpose and feeling like you belong. I understood it. I really did, and I have a good deal of respect for Julie for being willing to read to them even though other options were available.

Taking a seat in the rear of the room, I listened while Julie read a sweet little story about an Amish widow who had lost her husband in a tragic buggy accident and finds love again in the new blacksmith who had recently moved into her community. Now I'm all for a good romance story, but I needed a little more passion and sex than this Amish tale was offering up. Like skin-on-skin contact and long, hot, sweaty encounters on an abandoned beach just as the sun is setting, accentuating every curve and every muscle. Preferably with a mature woman and a much younger man with a body of steel and a tongue he knew how to use!

Anyway, I listened for as long as Julie continued reading, probably a couple of chapters, which is about how long it took for a majority of the residents to nod off, signaling a good stopping point for the day. Whether any of the residents would remember the story when she picked it back up next time this group met was anyone's guess. Even I, at a sprightly sixty-seven, had trouble remembering what I had read the day before.

As Julie closed the book, I assisted her in reawakening those who had fallen asleep to let them know that story time was over for the day. Some were harder to awaken than others, and Julie had to use a whistle to coax the last of the slumbering beauties into consciousness. But eventually, we got them on their way, and I accompanied Julie back to her office. I tried my best to act as casually as I could, not wanting to raise her suspicions by indicating I had some sort of ulterior motive.

When we arrived, Julie took the seat behind her desk and closed her eyes. I asked her if she was okay, but she didn't immediately respond. I thought about getting up and slapping her in the face to see if I'd get a reaction, but that seemed a little rude. Plus, my plan was to butter her up a bit to get her to talk about Scott, and slapping her probably would have made that plan more difficult to execute. So, I sat back and waited for little miss princess to open her eyes again. Which she did, five minutes later.

"Where did you go?" I asked.

"Oh, to a place where there is no sadness. To a place where everyone gets to live their dreams and there's no war or sickness or death."

"Sounds like there'd be a lot of really old people there," I laughed. "Not unlike Springtime Pastures!"

She wasn't amused by my little joke, so I asked her why she seemed so wistful. I didn't get much of a response, so I barreled right along with my plan to ask her questions whose answers would involve names and/or numbers. There wasn't much I could do if his password had a special character in it, though. I'd just have to hope he didn't include one.

"Sometimes I find it helpful to talk about a person I've recently lost," I said. "It's part of the grieving process, at least for me. So, tell me a little about Scott. Fill in the story of his life, since my copy is missing a few chapters."

"What would you like to know?" Julie asked half-heartedly.

"Everything!" I exclaimed. "Did he have any brothers or sisters? Any children from previous marriages or relationships? Do you by any chance know his driver's license number? Or maybe his social security number? What about pets? I didn't see any pets when we were at his house. Did he have any previous pets whom he loved and adored? What about his first love? What was her name? Did his high school have a mascot? What about previous addresses? Do you know the addresses of the last couple of places he lived? Specific streets and street numbers? Did he have any favorite sports figures he followed? What about gambling? Did he ever play the lottery? Did he have any lucky numbers? What year was he born?"

She looked at me like I had lost my mind. I tried to explain that I wanted to do a collage as a way to memorialize Scott and needed as much information as she could provide me. I thought I sold the lie pretty convincingly, and for a moment, she looked like she was going to cooperate. But only for a moment. Her eyes narrowed, and then she called me out.

"I shouldn't have allowed you to take Scotty's laptop. You're trying to figure out his password. Where is it now? I need to return it to his house."

"Even after I rolled around on top of it completely naked?" I asked, grasping at straws trying to dissuade her. "I'm sure there's all sorts of body prints on it now. Look, I understand what you're saying. I really do. But I'm not giving you the laptop. If I did that, I'd never hear the end of it from the other ladies."

"Why do you care about what they'd have to say? Aren't you supposed to be leaving here in a couple of weeks anyway? Isn't your house almost done being rebuilt?"

"Because I'm a woman of my word. I told them I'd find a way to gain access to his computer, and that's exactly what I'm going to do. With or without your help."

"Hmm," she said as she began riffling through one of her desk drawers.

She took out a pad from one of them and flipped it open to one of the interior pages.

"Yep, exactly as I thought," she said. "You're past due for another room inspection. I think now is as good a time as any to do a thorough inventory of your premises."

As she started to get up from her seat, I began to panic. Even though I was still pretty spry for my age, I knew I wouldn't win a tug of war with Julie if she happened to find the laptop. I hastily opened my pocketbook and searched for something, anything I could use as a weapon. When my hand made contact with the can of pepper spray I was hoping was in there, I paused for a split second. Was I really about to pepper-spray Julie? Was this how I wanted to get kicked out of Springtime Pastures? Because I surely would be. Assaulting a staff member unless you had a dementia diagnosis was a strict no-no and earned you a one-way ticket out of here.

But I had to come up with some way to stall her. Some way to keep her preoccupied until I could get up to my cell and move the laptop to a safer location. Every fiber of my being was telling me not to let Julie get a hold of that laptop. I couldn't explain why. I just knew that I needed to keep her away from it. If Julie was as invested in finding out what may have happened to Scott as the other ladies were, she'd be doing everything she could to help us gain access. Instead, she was working against us, and I didn't know why.

Yes, she allowed us to search Scott's house, but what was the point? Why take us over there and then stonewall our attempts to investigate further? What could she possibly have to gain by impeding our progress? And how in the hell did she grow enough brain cells overnight to pick up on my earlier attempts to extract password-related information from her? It's not that I thought Julie was dumb, but in the six months I've known her, she's never given me the slightest reason to think she was of above average intelligence.

"Julie," I said as calmly as I could, "the hand I currently have in my pocketbook is clasped around a can of pepper spray."

I wasn't going to use it on her; I had made that decision. But I wanted her to think I was capable of doing so if pushed. Well, her eyes bugged out of her head in disbelief, and she sat back down. I wondered if merely threatening to attack a staff member was sufficient grounds for my eviction, but she seemed to be considering her options. Actually, she looked like a trapped rat, darting her gaze from one side of the room to the other, looking for another way out. It was almost endearing to watch. I had her, and she knew it.

"Now, I'm going to back out of this room very slowly. If you know what's good for you, you'll stay put in your seat until I'm gone. I don't want to have to hurt you. I like you. I really do. In fact, you're one of the kindest people I've met here.

When I finally do flee this coop, I'm going to recommend you be promoted."

I didn't know what she could be promoted to, but I figured there must be something else she was qualified to do here.

"I thought we were friends," Julie responded in a slightly mournful tone. "But friends don't threaten to pepper-spray their other friends."

"Every friendship has its limits," I explained. "Look, it's obvious you don't want me to hack into Scott's laptop. But you haven't explained why. If you really loved Scott, and I still have my doubts about that, wouldn't you want to do everything in your power to find out what happened to him? Why a perfectly healthy man was found face down and lifeless in a pool? We might not find anything of use on the device, but what if we do? We don't have any reason to believe yet that the authorities will investigate Scott's death. We don't know what the autopsy will show, if one is even performed. But we have a chance to figure this out ourselves, or at least discover some clues that might point us in the right direction."

I let my words sink in for a moment, giving Julie a chance to process for herself that it was in our mutual interest to gain access to the contents on Scott's laptop. And then it hit me. She *knew* what was on Scott's laptop and was trying to protect the contents from me and the other ladies. What I wasn't sure of yet was whether the contents pointed to a crime or were of a more personal nature she was trying to keep hidden.

Think about it. She knew where the laptop was. When we asked her last night about it, she could have simply said she didn't know. But she went right into the kitchen and retrieved it for us. And then she made an attempt at guessing the password. Maybe she didn't actually know it? Maybe she did. She then expressed her reservations regarding our confiscation of the laptop from the premises, but she didn't put up much of a fight. I mean, sure, she was outnumbered four to one, but we're all somewhere between thirty and fifty years older than she is. She could have outrun us. She could have gotten back to her car and sped off with the laptop, leaving us stranded. But she didn't. She *allowed* me to take the laptop and bring it back here to my cell.

"Tell me, Julie," I said, hoping that the hunch I was operating under would bear fruit, "are there any pictures of you on this laptop?"

Julie didn't respond right away but took her time instead, probably trying to determine how much information she was willing to divulge. Either way, I knew I was on to something here, and I was determined to press forward.

"I don't know what you mean," she lied.

"Yes, you do," I said, and then I explained the reasoning behind my belief that she had something to hide or protect. "Whatever it is that you're trying to keep buried, is it more important than getting to the bottom of what happened to Scott? Listen, I'm not saying we're going to find all of the answers we're looking for on that device, but it's the best place we have to start."

She bit her lip nervously and averted her gaze, obviously trying to decide if there was any way out of this situation for her. But with a loving yet firm grasp of her hand, I communicated that it was time to unburden herself and that I would stand by her no matter what. Together, we would face her truth.

"It's, well, you know that activities directors at retirement communities don't get paid a lot, right?" she asked.

"I figured as much. Go on."

"And water aerobics instructors at retirement communities don't get paid a lot either," she added.

I nodded and decided not to divulge all the details Rebecca and I had uncovered about those large bank transfers into Scott's account until I knew where Julie was headed with this. Scott wasn't in any sort of desperate financial situation based on that forensic accounting work we had done. But Julie had certainly piqued my curiosity.

"Oh, it's all so shameful!" she cried. "I'm so embarrassed now, but I really needed the cash. It was the only way I could pay my rent."

"What did you do?"

"We, Scott and I, well, we filmed ourselves."

Now, here's one of those moments when you have to make a split decision. Do you come right out and ask the question that's burning on your mind? Or do you play innocent and pretend to have no idea why their cinematic exploits are at all relevant to the topic at hand? I chose the former.

"Let me see if I have the complete picture here. You two filmed yourselves having sex, or perhaps performing sexual acts on each other, and then put the video up online on some sort of pornographic website. Oh, and the video is stored on that laptop, which is why you've been so determined to stop me and the other ladies from gaining access. Does that sound about right?"

"Videos."

"You mean multiple videos of you two getting it on?" I asked, not really needing a reply at this point. "Well, when this is all over, I want you to teach me how to make some of those videos for myself. I've been known to turn a head or two in my day, and I'm sure there's got to be men out there, or even women, who have a wrinkle fetish. I'd finally be able to live out my retirement in the digs and comfort I feel I'm entitled to!"

This actually got a laugh out of Julie, which helped cut the tension a bit. I had one more question for her, though, and that was why she let us take the laptop in the first place. She explained that she had planned to sneak into my cell and retrieve it while I was at breakfast but had been sidelined by an unruly resident who kept insisting his underwear wasn't visible when it was clear that he had put them on *over* his pants for all to see.

"Okay, Julie. How about this? You and I will deal with the laptop together. We won't allow any of the other ladies to gain access. We will delete whatever videos you and I determine aren't relevant to our investigation, and that'll be the end of it. Do we have a deal?"

She was relieved and agreed to the terms I had laid out. Unfortunately, she also said that she really didn't know the password to Scott's laptop, so I was pretty much back to square one. Well, almost.

12

Julie and I had arranged to get together after her shift ended for the day to see if we could figure out the password based on her knowledge of Scott. But just to be on the safe side, I removed the laptop from my cell and locked it up in my car. I was mostly convinced that Julie's story about naked videos stored on the device was true, but *mostly* doesn't cut it in my book. If she was deceiving me, I wanted to make sure the laptop wasn't in my cell in case of a surprise inspection. And I wasn't about to sit around for the rest of the day to thwart her if that's what she decided to do.

I had made arrangements to meet up with Rebecca to go over all of the evidence we had collected on her phone. We also needed to figure out a way to make the pictures and documents available and easily accessible to the four of us. None of us was particularly tech savvy, and some of us were downright technophobes. Not me, of course. But you know, Anna Lee and to a lesser extent Lanie.

We decided that our best bet in getting some expert help in creating a repository of sorts was to go to the public library and ask for assistance. Gone were the days of libraries being run by little old ladies in floral-print dresses and beehive hairdos telling everyone to keep their voices down. No, public librarians were much more dynamic, interactive, and engaged with their patrons, offering any help they could. They were also far more technologically knowledgeable than their frumpy forebears could have ever dreamt of becoming.

Rebecca did ask me on the way if I'd had any luck with the laptop, and while I told her that I hadn't, I explained that I did have a plan. Thankfully, she dropped the subject. I wasn't sure I was ready to divulge my earlier attempt with Julie and the revelations that followed. I started wondering, though, if maybe one of the public librarians could teach me how to make some of those erotic videos Julie was so desperate to hide. I mean, public librarians are people too. I'm sure some of them have porn habits of their own, and perhaps a few have gone down the same path Julie and Scott had. They don't get paid much either. Maybe there was a whole website devoted to public librarian porn stars! Like "librariansgettinglaid.com" or something.

Upon entering the library, however, our hopes were somewhat dashed. The place was mobbed, and every staff member we could identify was busy with other patrons. While it warmed my heart to see the public library being used so heavily, I wasn't looking forward to having to wait around for help. Not that I had a particularly full social calendar for the day, but I was eager to get to work on this little project of ours. Rebecca, sensing my impatience, suggested that we go get a coffee and come back, but I told her it would probably be even busier by the time we returned as the day wore on.

We made our way over to the reference desk where a young librarian was on the phone, presumably with a patron. I wasn't getting the entire conversation, but it sounded like he was trying to tell the patron that, no, the patron couldn't use the library's mailing address for business purposes. The librarian then told the patron that, no, the patron couldn't use the library's street address either. When the librarian asked the patron about the nature of the business, whatever the patron said had the librarian ending the call in short order. I later found out that the patron was trying to start a gay escort service and needed an address for tax purposes that his wife wouldn't find out about.

"Hello, ladies," the librarian said once he realized that we were staring at him, waiting for a greeting. "How can I help you today?"

"Well, we need some technological help. We're here on, um, some official business," I began, "and we're looking for a little bit of assistance in organizing our documentation."

"Official business?" he asked.

"Yes," Rebecca replied, "official business. We're investigating a possible murder, and we've collected some evidence and are now in need of a way to organize said evidence so that our entire investigative team can have easy access at any time. But it needs to be secure enough so that no one can gain unauthorized access."

The librarian looked at us suspiciously, and frankly, I couldn't blame him. Rebecca was far too honest about our purpose here. We really should have come up with a more plausible story ahead of time. Like, perhaps we'd had a recent family reunion and wanted to organize all of the shared photos, certificates, and other random digital memorabilia. The two of us certainly didn't look like we were in any way working for an official law enforcement agency or even a private eye for that matter. That I was wearing my "Screw the Government" T-shirt probably didn't help our case either.

"Look," I said, thinking quickly, "we didn't mention anything about investigating a *human* murder, now did we? My pet bird went missing from his cage, and well, I found a couple of feathers on the floor beneath. Plus, he's not smart enough to open his cage himself and fly away. So, we have pictures of a potential crime scene, plus we've interviewed the people who had access to my abode and have transcribed those interviews. We simply need to figure out a place in the clouds where we can store everything. Got it?"

"In the clouds?" he asked.

"She means in the cloud," Rebecca clarified unnecessarily, since I had deliberately added that little *s* to bolster the impression that we really needed help.

"So you're looking for some sort of cloud storage that you can upload your files to and give access only to those who you authorize? Do I have that right?" he asked.

I nodded, and the librarian swiveled his computer screen around so we could see what he was doing. He pulled up a couple of different options for us to look at, explaining the various features of each one. I was impressed that he seemed to know so much about cloud storage. Librarians really are the unsung heroes of our society. They know *everything*.

After working through the pros and cons of each of the services he identified for us, we settled on one called Cloudy Storage. I thought the name was tacky, but it had a generous amount of free storage space and had an app that we could all download to our phones or other devices for easy access. The librarian then helped Rebecca download said app on her phone so she could upload all the snapshots of evidence we took at Scott's house. He offered to do the uploads for us, but I politely declined on our behalf. If he got a look at any of the snapshots we had taken, he'd quickly realize we weren't investigating the possible murder of my imaginary pet bird.

We thanked the librarian and took a seat at one of the few empty tables to do the uploading. Rebecca wanted to get back to Springtime Pastures and do the uploading there, but I told her it would be better to stay put in case we needed any further help from the librarian. She reluctantly agreed, and we got to work. It took us a while to get the hang of it, but we eventually did, and before we knew it, we were more than halfway done uploading our evidence. We were so proud of ourselves, two senior ladies proving that we weren't too old to learn new tricks.

Once the uploads were done and we got my phone all hooked up to the Cloudy Storage system, we gathered our belongings and stood up to leave. But out of the corner of my eye, I spotted something that drew my attention. A man, a very familiar-looking man, was sitting at one of the computers with a child, perhaps his daughter? She might have been about ten years old. The man appeared to be helping his daughter with a project of some sort. Maybe doing a little bit of light research using age-appropriate websites or databases. Something about her, though, even from a distance, made me wonder about the girl. Her features. Her eyes, even from a distance. I knew those features. But I didn't know from where.

"Rebecca," I whispered as I tugged at her sleeve and pointed in the man's direction with my other hand. "Look over there."

"Don't tug on me. You break me; you buy me," she laughed.

"Shhh!" I said. "I don't want him to know we're looking his way."

"Whose way?"

"That man, sitting over there with that girl. If I didn't know better, I'd swear he was the man from that photo we found in Scott's album."

Rebecca took out her phone to start thumbing through the snapshots we had taken.

"No! The photo we actually confiscated. You know, the one with Scott and a distinguished-looking gentleman in a dimly lit restaurant? Damn, I wish I had thought to bring it along today. But either that man has a doppelganger wandering around or he and the man sitting at that computer over there are one and the same."

"Are you sure?" Rebecca asked, looking doubtfully at the man.

Was I absolutely sure? No. Was I pretty sure? Yes. I told Rebecca to sit back down while I came up with a plan to introduce myself to him. I needed something that wouldn't immediately arouse suspicions.

"Okay, I'm going in," I said a few moments later. "Cover me!"

"Cover you?" she asked rhetorically. "I wasn't aware that we were under sniper fire! I think you're letting this whole investigation go to your head. And to be honest, if anyone is going to go confront that man, shouldn't it be me? I'm the most even keeled among us."

"Even keeled, yes. But a master at deception? Well, I have my doubts. Simply put, you'll blow our cover."

"I will not!" she exclaimed, as several heads within our immediate vicinity started to turn in our direction.

"Lower your voice," I whispered, and she obliged. "Listen, here's the plan. I'm going to go over there and pretend to need some help with my phone. Since the library is so busy today, hopefully the man will be willing to lend a helping hand to this poor, confused elderly lady. I'll tell him that for some reason I can't get my phone to unlock. Like maybe I forgot my password."

"And he'll take one look at you, hold your phone up to your face, and let the Face ID unlock the phone for you."

"So what? It's an in. And then I can thank him profusely while working in a couple of innocent questions to gain some information. Like his name and where he lives, all under the guise of wanting to send him a fruit basket to thank him for his help."

"Goodness, no wonder your daughter put you in a home," Rebecca laughed. "That's got to be one of the craziest plans I've heard in a long time."

"You have a better one?" I asked.

"Well, no. But give me a moment. I'll think of something."

"Look, I know you're supposed to be an expert or something in the art of thinking, but right now, your well of knowledge runneth dry. Stay put until I get back."

I left Rebecca where she sat, before she could get another word in edgewise, and made my way over to where the gentleman and his presumed daughter were sitting. They appeared not to notice me at first, their gazes fixed on the computer screen, so I cleared my throat to get their attention.

They both looked up at me, he with a slightly perturbed expression and she with a hint of curiosity in her eyes.

"I'm so sorry to bother the two of you," I said, laying it on pretty thick. "But I seem to have locked myself out of my phone, and I was wondering if you might be willing to help me out. I'm afraid I'm not very tech savvy."

"Um, ma'am," the gentleman began, "I don't mean to be rude, but isn't there a staff member somewhere around who could help you? My daughter and I are very busy working on a report for her science class, and we don't have a whole lot of time."

With every bit of restraint I could muster, I politely explained that all of the library staff members were busy helping other patrons at the moment. He suggested that I wait until one of them was free, while giving his daughter a warning glance not to get involved. I said that I wasn't sure I could wait that long. I made up an excuse about having one of those continuous glucose monitors for diabetes and that I needed access to my phone so I could scan the device and get my current sugar reading. I lied and said I wasn't feeling well, but that I couldn't tell whether my blood sugar was high or low. I then might have implied that if I guessed incorrectly, I could end up in the hospital.

"Daddy," the girl said, "I bet I can help this lady. Isn't Mom always telling us to be kind and helpful in public? Like because it helps her image?"

"Never mind," her father said, "I'll handle this. You just keep reading that website we've got pulled up."

The father stood from his seat, grabbed the phone out of my hand, and as Rebecca predicted, held it up to my face. The phone unlocked, and I made a concerted effort to look genuinely thankful for his assistance.

"I don't know why it wasn't working for me," I lied. "Sometimes these devices can be so temperamental."

"I know, right?" the daughter said. "Sometimes when my grandma leans over hers and her face droops, it doesn't recognize her."

I wasn't too thrilled with that explanation, but I played along, thankful that this child gave me an excuse for my faked phone problem. You'd think these devices would be smart enough to work for a woman of any age, no matter how much her face distends downward when leaning over.

"Now, if you don't mind," the father said as he averted his gaze from mine and sat back down to face the computer.

"Oh no, not at all, but sir, maybe there's something I could do in return for your incredibly generous, magnanimous help. If you give me your name and address, I could send you a fruit basket or maybe a box of gourmet candies or chocolates."

The daughter perked up at this, but her father declined to provide the requested information. He held his hand up as his daughter started to speak, and glared at me. He wanted me to leave.

"Okay, but one more thing," I said as I opened the Cloudy Storage app on my phone and scanned through its contents.

I found one of the pictures of Scott in a Speedo from his Olympics days and held the phone in front of the father's face.

"A dear friend of mine recently passed away unexpectedly. Do you know this man?"

13

The father looked like he had seen a ghost; I kid you not. He began gathering up his belongings and told his daughter that she could finish her research at home. I pressed him again, but he ignored me. I thought about showing the snapshot of Scott to the daughter to see if she might have recognized him, but since he was so scantily clad, I didn't want to risk being charged with some sort of indecent exposure incident involving a minor.

As the father and daughter headed toward the exit, I motioned for Rebecca to get up and meet me outside. I was going to follow them, all the way to their car. Problem was, I shouldn't have been so hot on their heels. The father broke into a jog and commanded his daughter to follow suit. Well, I tried to keep up with them, but as they picked up speed and I tried to keep pace, a damn charley horse came out of nowhere and arrested my forward momentum. Rebecca caught up to me a moment later, and I pointed in the direction of the escapees.

"Stop them! Or at least get the license plate number off their car!" I said, thinking as quickly as I could on how to salvage the situation.

She looked at me like I had snot coming out of my nose or something. But after a slight pause, she headed in their direction and took out her phone. I figured she was going to try to take a picture of the plate, probably wise, since it would take her longer to get a pad and pen out of her purse to write it down. I watched in suspense as Rebecca got closer to the car, but the father and daughter were already inside. The next thing I knew, he backed the car out of the parking space, nearly running Rebecca over in the process, and sped away. Rebecca reacted quickly enough to avoid being hit and managed to attempt a snapshot of the plate on the rebound.

I, however, was on the ground a moment later, doubled over in pain, with Rebecca and two of the library staff members standing over me with concerned expressions on their faces. *How embarrassing*, I thought. A third staff member came out with an office chair on wheels and asked if I needed some help getting up while we all waited for the paramedics to arrive.

"You called an ambulance?" I asked, turning my gaze toward Rebecca. "That wasn't necessary."

"I didn't," she said. "The staff must have."

The staff member with the chair said that it was standard protocol anytime an elderly patron fell on the premises. I mean, I knew I was no spring chicken, and yes, I've referred to myself as an elderly lady when it suited my purposes. But as far as I was concerned, I was still middle aged. Sixty-seven is the new fifty-six in my book! And with minimal help, I managed to get into the chair.

"Please send them away when they arrive," I said to the staff members. "I'm fine."

"Can't," one of them responded. "You fell here; you get checked out here."

"The only thing that should be checked out here is a good book!" I said.

Rebecca shook her head, though I wasn't sure if she disapproved of my little joke or of the impending fiasco I was about to cause when I refused the paramedics' service. And as if on cue, they arrived in full force, sirens blazing. This was so embarrassing. But for better or worse, Rebecca took charge of the situation and explained what had happened and how I ended up on the ground. They did a once-over on me, and after I declined their oh-so-generous offer to take me to the hospital for some X-rays to make sure nothing was broken, they left. The library staff then insisted on walking us back to our car to make sure I got in without falling again, and we were on our way a moment later.

"Do you want to stop somewhere and grab a bite?" Rebecca asked as she turned out of the library's parking lot. "I'll treat."

"Well, in that case, I'd love to. By the way, did you have a chance to look at the snapshot you took of the license plate? Can you make out the number?"

"It's a little blurry, and I was farther away than I would have liked. I can't quite make it out, but maybe someone with younger eyes than either of us could take a look. Or maybe someone who knows how to sharpen digital images."

"I'd ask Julie, but she doesn't know how to sharpen much of anything," I laughed.

"Don't short-change her, Millie. She's not stupid. Believe me. I know stupid. Not everyone who goes to an Ivy League school has a brain. I've attempted to teach more stupid kids whose parents had enough money to donate buildings or create endowed professorships than I care to admit. Julie isn't stupid. She might not always make the best decisions for herself, and she might be a little slow to get a joke when one is made, but she's got some horsepower up there in that head of hers."

"Well, I've known her longer than you have, but perhaps I may have overlooked something," I offered as I searched for a way to steer the conversation in another direction.

What I hadn't realized was that while Rebecca and I were chatting, she had piloted the car toward the nearest donut shop. My mood instantly brightened. Whoever said donuts weren't a cure-all for whatever was troubling you obviously hadn't tasted any from this particular establishment. It's a one-of-a-kind, family-run business. They bake their donuts fresh every single day. Plus, they always have my favorite flavor, maple frosted.

"I know you pretty well, too," Rebecca said as she pulled into a parking spot. "Better than you think. You've spent the last six months at Springtime Pastures not really trying to make friends or connections. Maybe you've made a few half-hearted attempts, but nothing serious. You figure you're only there for six months, so what's the point, right? Maybe you've unwittingly made a friend in Julie. But beyond her? Who else? You're clearly an extroverted soul. There are plenty of us in the community who would have liked the chance to become a part of your life, even after you leave."

She had my attention, barely. The smell of donuts was wafting in our direction from the open door of the shop and through the car window.

"We're not all like Lanie and Anna Lee," she continued. "And if I'm being completely honest, they're not really all that bad. Sure, they both put on a façade, and in Lanie's case a particularly thick one at that, but think about it this way. There's a part of each of us that is still who we were when we were children. Can't you just see a little Anna Lee holding court and pretending to be a queen, tiara and all? And Lanie as a little girl trying to be the most popular kid on the block to hide her insecurity?"

"So, are you suggesting that I look at both of them as if they were still little girls, simply trying to cope with whatever problems they have in the best way they know how?" I asked, impressed with Rebecca's psychoanalytic skills.

"Something like that," she confirmed. "I'm not saying that I'm the best of friends with them, but we all care about each other. You could have been a part of that. You still can. Even Anna Lee thinks very highly of you, though I doubt she'd admit as much if anyone flat out asked her. At least not yet. Yes, I know she can be a bit pretentious with her little tea socials and proclamations, but underneath that veneer of southern aristocracy, there's a genuinely good person. Very old school for sure, but not so stuck in her ways that she can't make minor adjustments for those she cares about."

I asked her as we got out of the car if she had any insights into what Lanie thought of me. She said Lanie admired my independence and my general "couldn't give two shits" attitude. I supposed that admiration had its limits, though, since she had accused me of killing poor Scott more than once over the last few days. Maybe she was just venting her frustration at not being able to save him herself. Even if she had gotten there first, and let's say for argument's sake, she had witnessed him falling into the pool unconscious, it was unlikely that she would have been able to do anything but scream her head off.

Lamenting the fact that this donut shop didn't have a drive-through window, we entered and got in line behind a mother and her five unruly kids. All I could think was that if this mother thought that giving her five out-of-control children donuts would somehow calm them down, she was in for a rude awakening. They'd be bouncing off the walls within minutes, and my "couldn't give two shits" attitude might inspire me to explain to the mother where she went wrong in her plans for the day.

As we continued to wait while each of the mother's five children went back and forth on which flavor donut they wanted, I asked Rebecca if she really thought there was a chance in hell of me becoming friends with Lanie. She reminded me that Lanie was really a very lonely person, and that if I wanted to make inroads with her, all I had to do was reach out. Well, the problem with that plan was that I had indeed reached out before, and I didn't particularly like the results I had gotten. There was that one night we went out for drinks not long after I moved in, but that was it. She never asked to make plans with me after that. Maybe she was embarrassed about revealing the true nature of her children's problems and that the image of the perfect life she tried so desperately to portray was a mirage.

"Let me ask you this," I said. "How do you get along with Lanie? You two are polar opposites."

"It sure does seem that way, doesn't it? Well, I think for me, it's because I have a lot of sympathy for her. You know about her husband's wandering eye, right? Well, my ex-husband was the same way. Goodness knows I spent years trying to fix our marriage, but I couldn't. He had this complex, like he wanted to be the dominant partner. He couldn't dominate me, and if I'm being completely honest, he didn't measure up, either. We weren't equals, professionally speaking, and that bothered him a great deal. He always worked, but never in a professional job. He didn't have a college degree."

"Is that why you never had children with him?" I asked.

"Precisely. I knew our marriage wasn't on solid ground, and I didn't feel it was fair to raise children in such an environment. I wasn't one of those women who thought that having children would fix everything. It rarely works out that way. Anyway, he looked for women who gave him that sense of superiority he so desperately craved. When one of them gave him a sexually transmitted disease, I had finally had enough and kicked him out."

The mother with the five unruly kids turned her head in our direction with a disapproving look. She asked us not to talk about topics that were inappropriate for her children's innocent little ears. I told her she ought to have better sense than to feed her amped up children a bunch of sugar-laden donuts. She said that what she fed her kids was none of my business. I responded by pointing out that if she was so offended by the parental advice I was offering, then perhaps she shouldn't be taking her kids out in public at all. She started to say something, but Rebecca cut her off, apologizing on our behalf, and settled the matter.

I'm not usually one to criticize others' parenting choices. I don't mind speaking my opinion as Rebecca pointed out, but even I know where to draw the line. I was a little shaken by my reaction to this woman. Granted, I probably wouldn't have said anything if she hadn't spoken first about the inappropriateness of the conversation Rebecca and I were having. But I still could have shown more self-control. Were her kids really bothering me? No, they weren't. I guess it just goes to show you that no matter how old you get, you still make mistakes. I thought about offering to pay for their donuts as a gesture of good will but decided against it. It was better to let the cards lie where they fell.

We ordered our donuts once the mother and her children were out of the way and then sat at a nearby table to enjoy our treat.

"Rebecca," I began, "far be it from me to judge, given that I raised my daughter as a single mother and still to this day have no idea who her biological father was, but why did you marry your husband? I mean, well, didn't it ever occur to you that your differences in educational and professional attainment might cause problems?"

"I see what you're saying. You'd think that because I was a professor of logic, it would have been crystal clear to me that it wouldn't work out. But we were in love. And we had to fight for our love. He wasn't Jewish. My parents didn't approve, and neither did his. I think, in a way, that's what drew us together more than anything else. We were both rebelling against our families and our faiths. Or at least twisted versions of our faiths."

"Did your parents ever come around?" I asked.

"They did eventually, at least while things were still good between me and my ex. I think they realized that either they had to let go of their antiquated notions regarding interfaith marriages or they were going to lose their daughter. However, once they found out about the cheating, he was dead to them, and once we were divorced, they sat shiva. They actually sat shiva for him."

"Remind me what shiva is?" I asked, a little embarrassed.

"It's the Jewish ritual of mourning," she explained.

"Oh, right," I said, as if I had known but had forgotten. "How long have you been divorced?"

"Twenty-five years. Funny how it seems like only yesterday while also feeling like it's a lifetime ago. I never remarried. Never felt the urge to. I created a life for myself that I found very satisfying. Teaching students, giving lectures, reengaging in my own Judaism, taking care of my parents before they died. I had a very fulfilling life."

"I don't think I've ever asked you this before," I said, "but what brought you down to North Carolina? Why not stay up North where you had built your life?"

"One too many nor'easters," she laughed. "I didn't want to deal with another cold winter, shoveling my driveway every other week, putting on layers and layers of clothing simply to walk out my front door."

"Sounds dreadful! I've lived here all my life and have often thought about moving away somewhere more in line with my personality and my interests. I might even sell my house once it's done being rebuilt and move out West. But it's an easy life here. Hard to uproot yourself, though I suppose you know that better than I do."

"You're never too old to try something new," she said. "I don't regret my move here for a single day."

That gave me some hope for the future.

14

Rebecca dropped me off back at B-Block after our little donut run, and I went upstairs to my cell to figure out what to do next. I needed to collect my thoughts after the day's events. It was bothering me to no end that I had that man from the photograph in my sights but still didn't know who he was, how he and Scott knew each other, or whether he might in some way be connected to Scott's death. That last seemed pretty far-fetched to me, but I couldn't quite square away the fact that he ran away when I asked if he knew him.

I started running through the possibilities, each more outlandish than the last. Was he a former coach of Scott's? Maybe a business partner in some sort of failed joint venture? Perhaps a friend of the family who had been cut off for some reason? Maybe even an older brother? Perhaps his mother had gotten pregnant by another man before marrying Scott's father? None of it made any sense to me. I was missing something. Problem was, I didn't know what.

And then there was the matter of the license plate number on the man's car. Rebecca had uploaded the snapshot she took to the Cloudy Storage, so I had access to it on my own phone now. I pulled up the image, hoping maybe I'd be able to make out the letters and numbers, but I couldn't. The image was definitely blurry, and my eyes were apparently no better than Rebecca's. I was going to have to find someone to help me clear the image up, if that was even possible.

Fixing myself an afternoon snack of cheese and crackers, I took a seat in front of the TV, hoping that a little mindless entertainment might help clear my head a bit. B-Block had its own unique package of cable channels that supposedly catered to the interests of most of the residents here. I wasn't so sure I agreed. What did residents in a retirement home need with multiple home and garden channels? It's not like we had any freedom to redecorate our cells. There was the obligatory selection of channels named after that greeting card company, of course. If you like sappy movies, then you're in luck. If you like the hardcore stuff, you're screwed. A couple of news channels, the local channels, the classic movie channel, and a few other odds and ends rounded out the lineup.

I turned to the classic movie channel, hoping maybe there'd be a Bette Davis movie on. Maybe one of her earlier pictures before she entered her horror flick phase. Something a bit more uplifting. Unfortunately, Bette Davis did not grace my

TV screen. Instead, a political thriller from the early sixties was on. I had seen it many years ago, but couldn't remember all the details. I watched it for about thirty minutes, enough to jog my memory. The plot went something like this: a young senator gets blackmailed and ultimately ends his life because he's about to be outed as a homosexual. Pretty racy stuff for the early sixties.

Anyway, once I got bored with the movie, I flipped the channel a few more times but didn't find anything else worth watching. Looking at the clock, I decided I had enough time to take a little nap before dinner. Figuring that a bit of shut-eye would do me some good, I undressed and got into my bed. But wouldn't you know it, my phone rang. I debated letting it go to voicemail, but a little voice inside my head told me to answer the call.

"Hello?" I asked, trying to hide my annoyance.

"Millie? It's Chessy."

"Oh, hi, Chessy," I said. "How are you doing? Wait, how did you get my number? I don't recall giving it to you."

"Dear, if you don't want bedazzled crazy ladies such as myself calling you without warning, you might want to take your number off of your website."

It took me longer than it should have to realize she must have googled me and found the website I had paid someone to create for me when I started my herbal supplement side hustle business. The site was very vague, referring mostly to natural remedies for common conditions such as arthritis, nausea, glaucoma, etc. Enough to ensure my visitors had an understanding of what I was providing without actually spelling it out. The site turned out to be a dud, though, generating very few potential customers, and I had nearly forgotten all about it.

"What are you doing right now?" she asked.

"I was just about to take a nap. Wanna join me?" I asked, figuring it was my turn to throw *her* off a little.

"Thank you, dear, for the offer, but I'll have to pass on that. I like my women the same way I like my men: firm bodies, amply sized extremities, and far too young to be receiving social security checks. I'm afraid you don't qualify."

Touché, I thought. Well, it was worth a try.

"Fine, if you're not interested in the company of an experienced woman, then to what do I owe the pleasure of your untimely call?" I asked.

"I wanted to check in with you to see how you're coming along with the laptop. What else would I be calling about?"

So, I went over the details of the events of the day since I left her in the dining room, still talking to her silverware. She sounded optimistic that I'd be able to figure out the password to the laptop. When I asked her if she knew anything about working with digital images, specifically clearing them up, she said she'd be happy to help if she could.

"Send the picture my way, and then come on down to my room in a few," she said. "We'll see what we can do. My email address is bedazzledcrazylady at, umm, something."

"You don't remember what service you use for your email?" I asked incredulously.

"Well, just send it to all the major providers, and one of your messages is bound to get to me. How many people out there could possibly have the same first part of their email address?"

I didn't even want to speculate on how many bedazzled crazy ladies there were in the world. Knowing that even one existed was more than enough for me.

"All right, I'll send it in a few moments. What cell number are you in?"

"Cell number? Look at your caller ID," she responded.

"No, I meant, what room are you in?" I clarified.

"Oh, I see. Funny. Room 327. See you in a bit."

I ended the call, sent the snapshot of the license plate to as many bedazzledcrazylady email addresses as I could come up with, and reluctantly put my clothes back on. I wasn't convinced Chessy would be able to help with the image, but what did I have to lose? I mean, other than a long-deserved nap. Minutes later she opened the door to her cell for me.

Taking a look around her abode, which was much larger than mine, I was struck by this sense that everything was just a little bit off. A painting of two cats cuddling each other hung ever so slightly crookedly on the far wall between the two windows. The blinds on one window were completely open, but the blinds on the other window were partially shut. The TV wasn't quite centered atop the stand on which it stood. The sofa was sticking out a bit on one side. A tattered rug was stuck halfway under the coffee table. And on each end table bracketing the sofa was a lamp. The bases were the same, but the shades were different.

"All part of the act," she assured me as she watched my gaze wander around the living room and dining area. "Well, mostly. I'm not what you would call a conformist. If I had my life to do over again, I would have been an artist. I'd have given Picasso a run for his money!"

"You know, if you want to avoid ending up in that memory care unit your daughter is threatening to throw you into, perhaps you should tone things down a bit," I suggested.

"I'll take that under advisement," she said, though I wasn't sure I believed her.

We took a seat at her dining room table where Chessy had her laptop set up. She asked me if I wanted anything to drink, and when I asked for a vodka straight up, she delivered! I was only kidding—sort of. I asked her how she managed to hide her contraband booze. She explained that all she had to do was start opening her door naked when staff members came by to check on her, and no one ever intruded again. I suggested that that might be playing into her daughter's determination that she needed a higher level of care than was offered in B-Block. She reluctantly conceded the point. I then asked her how she managed to keep staff out of her room when she wasn't in it, like when she was visibly playing bingo downstairs.

"Oh, that's easy," Chessy responded. "I set a little motion-activated trap for them. One of those alarm systems that run totally wirelessly."

"But won't they confiscate it? Haven't they?"

"Oh, yes, eventually they do. But I simply replace it. I have the app on my phone to control it, and I can very easily add a replacement sensor if one is taken. My daughter supplies me with them because, well, it's part of the act. You know, 'bedazzled crazy lady thinks there are intruders in her bedroom every night.'"

"I'm surprised they haven't kicked you out by now. I'm sure those devices go against policy here. And how do you explain to your daughter that you keep losing the sensors?"

"Simple. I placed one in the trash can right before she stopped by for one of her visits. She put two and two together and figured that I was throwing them away, not realizing what they were, like in a moment of delusion. And since I carry my own trash bags to the trash drop down the hall, she assumes I just throw them away all together."

"And she hasn't caught on?" I asked.

"No, of course not. She genuinely thinks I've lost my marbles," Chessy laughed. "That's why she wants to lock me up and throw away the key."

"Well, we won't let her," I said as I grabbed Chessy's hand in solidarity. "Worst comes to worst, you can live with me at my house once it's done being rebuilt."

I didn't know what the hell I was saying. I had already taken a couple of sips of the vodka, so maybe I wasn't in my right mind. But how could I have invited her to live with me? I barely knew her!

"Thank you, dear, for that very generous offer. But I'm not so sure a single house has room for the two of us. Let's face it, we've both got larger than life personalities, and sooner or later, one of us would probably take a skillet to the back of the other's head."

She was right, but still, she could have softened the blow a bit. She didn't even pause before answering. When someone offers to let you live in their house, the least you can do is pretend to seriously consider it rather than rejecting it out of hand. At the same time, I was a little relieved that I hadn't boxed myself into a corner so carelessly.

"I'm still surprised the staff here hasn't evicted you, though. They're usually so persnickety about the rules. How did you, or perhaps your daughter, convince them to let you stay even after your multiple infractions?" I asked.

"I tip well. Too well. It's part of the act. You know, bedazzled crazy lady gives a twenty-dollar tip to the maintenance man who changes a light bulb for her. That kind of thing."

"But if you ran through all your money taking care of your late husband, where are you getting the cash from?" I asked.

"Simple. I have an investment account that my daughter doesn't know about. It's not nearly enough for me to live on, but it provides me with a couple hundred a month in spending money. And before you ask, yes, they send me a check, and no, I don't have any means of getting to a bank to cash the check since I'm not allowed to leave the premises. So…"

"Wait a sec," I interrupted. "You're not allowed to leave? I thought everyone was allowed to leave if they wanted to."

"Not when you're a dementia patient," she explained. "Anyway, I made an arrangement with Julie when I first moved in. I endorse the check over to her. She cashes the check, takes a modest cut for herself, and then brings me the rest of the money in twenty-dollar bills. Oh, and she helps me with the booze too."

"So what you're saying is, you're basically bribing the staff to look the other way when you do something you're not supposed to do," I reasoned.

"Pretty much!" she confirmed. "Anyway, let's get to the business of looking at that image you sent me. Maybe I can sharpen it enough so you can make out the letters and numbers on the plate."

"One more thing before we begin," I said as I fished a couple of pill bottles out of my pocketbook. "Do you know where I can send these to be tested? I just want to be sure they're really what they're supposed to be."

"Good thinking," she said as she took the bottles from me. "I'll take care of it and let you know the results."

She found the image in her email, which was no small miracle, and then opened it up in a computer program I wasn't familiar with. I've never had a mind for technology, always mastering only what was absolutely necessary to get by. Who knows, maybe if I had been more adept, I could have become the queen pot granny of the East Coast!

I watched Chessy as she manipulated the image with more skill than any octogenarian should have possessed. She explained what she was doing, but I barely kept up. She tried changing the contrast of the image, with mixed results. She tried pixelating the image, also with mixed results. Then she tried using some sort of magic wand tool to eliminate everything from the image except for what looked like the digits on the plate. That didn't work, so she backtracked a bit. Finally, she used a color replacement tool to redo every individual pixel that might have been a part of a digit into a single hue. That mostly did the trick.

"Well, what do you think?" she asked, pleased with herself, as I took a look at the final product.

"Umm, well, I think I can make out most of the characters now. Still not sure if that first one is a 'B' or an 'E'. And the second number in the series, is that a '5' or a '6'?"

"I think that first letter is a 'B'. Not sure about that number," Chessy said.

"Well, okay. So that leaves us with B,M,H,9,5 or 6,9,3. And you're sure there's nothing else you can do to figure out that last digit that's still a little fuzzy?"

"I'm not a miracle worker, you know," she laughed.

"Perhaps not, but you're the next best thing!" I said as I gave her shoulders a squeeze. "One more thing. How do I look up a license plate number to see who it belongs to?"

15

As much as I appreciated Chessy's help, that help only went so far. She was unable to provide me with a reliable way to look up the owner of the license plate. She said there were a number of commercial services out there that might provide the information for a fee if I wanted to pay up. But even then, she couldn't guarantee that I'd get the identity of the current owner and said I was more likely to pull up past ownership information if the plate was no longer in service. Well, I knew it was still in service.

I did manage to find a state records website that would have provided me with all of the current information on the plate except for the name of the person it belonged to. Or at least, I thought I had. They, too, wanted me to pay a fee. But I had a better idea. Maybe a slightly, possibly illegal idea, but it was worth a try.

Grabbing my pocketbook, I went downstairs and out to my car, and slipped into the driver's seat. I took off and headed toward a street I knew had pretty wide lanes and decent shoulder space. You see, this is where having a car that's a little dented up really comes in handy! I pulled over, called for the police, and waited for them to arrive.

A few moments later, I heard a knock on my window, and I looked up into the most beautiful blue eyes I've ever seen. Those eyes sat in a strikingly handsome face, and for a second, I wondered if I'd have the nerve to pull off my plan. He was simply mesmerizing! After attempting to gather my wits about me, I lowered the window.

"Ma'am," the officer said. "Are you all right?"

"I-I think so," I stammered.

"Did you call the police to report an accident? A hit and run?" he asked in the most melodic southern drawl I think I've ever heard.

I couldn't quite place the accent, though. People not from the south tend to think that all southerners talk the same regardless of which state or region they're from. But that isn't the case. Anna Lee's accent is very Deep-South southern. Lanie, born and bred in Raleigh, sounds very different. Move on up to Virginia, and you begin to hear a slight change as well. As for me, I got rid of my native accent many years ago. Took a lot of practice and many hours of watching Hollywood daytime soaps, but I did it! As for this police officer, his accent genuinely stumped me. I had no idea where he was from originally.

"Umm, yes, I called to report an accident," I eventually responded.

"Would you like to get out of your car and tell me what happened?"

"If it's okay with you, I'd prefer not to get out of my car. I'm very shaken up. Very very shaken up. He came out of nowhere and sideswiped me. Just sideswiped me. He stopped his car several yards down the road, and then after a minute, he sped away."

"Okay, ma'am. Can you tell me where he hit you? Which side of the vehicle?"

I had to stop a moment and think. Which side had more dents? It should have occurred to me to look before I got in the car. *Damn*, I thought.

"It happened like this," I answered, making it up as I went along. "I was in the left lane, minding my business when this prick in a Benz comes barreling out of nowhere, gets a little too close to my car and manages to hit my right front fender."

The police officer walked around to the right side of my car to survey the damage for himself. I might have actually moaned a little when I caught a good look at his keister. Nothing better than a hot man with an ample rear end. Really filled out his pants. Technically speaking, he was probably young enough to be my grandson, but just barely. He motioned for me to roll down the passenger-side window, so I did.

"Ma'am," he said, "are you sure this is where he hit your car? I see a dent, well, a couple of dents, but I would have expected more damage to have occurred if he had hit this particular area while both cars were moving."

Okay, so I might have caused those dents myself, pulling my car into the garage and accidentally hitting a tall garden gnome that I was storing for a friend. I kept forgetting the damn thing was there. And since I used half of my garage for storage anyway, there wasn't room to move the gnome elsewhere. I'm not a hoarder, but I do have a habit of collecting things from time to time and, well, not getting rid of them. But only in my garage. My former garage, that is.

"I swear, that's where the prick hit me," I stated, trying for a believable tone but probably falling short.

"You said the guy was driving a Mercedes? What else can you tell me about him or the car? Were you able to identify the model of the car? What color was the car? Did the car look like a recent model or perhaps a bit older?"

As they say, the devil's in the details, and I had no details! If only I had gotten a better look at that man's car before he sped off from the library earlier, but I hadn't. All I had was a blurry image, mostly of the license plate, and I had no idea if the car was even a Benz to begin with. I knew it was silver, though, and that had to count for something!

"I don't know how old the car was. But I know it was silver," I offered.

"Okay, that's a start. Now what can you tell me about its driver?" he asked.

"Oh, he was about five-foot eleven, average build, brown hair, green eyes, not bad looking, but not as gorgeous as you are!" I said before thinking better of it.

"Ma'am, let's stick to the facts here. Now, something's bothering me. You said earlier that he only stopped his car for a moment after the collision before he sped off again. How were you able to get such a good look at him? You didn't mention him getting out of the car before. Did he?"

"Well, of course he did! He wanted to inspect the damage to his own car, I am sure," I lied.

"Okay, anything else you can tell me before I go back to my patrol car to begin the accident report?"

"Yes," I said as I reached for my pocketbook to take out my phone.

"Ma'am!" he yelled, startling me. "No sudden movements. Do not reach into your purse unless I tell you to do so!"

"Look, young man," I said, trying to play up the curmudgeonly grandmother vibe a bit. "There's no need to take that tone of voice with me! If there's something you want me to do or not do, try asking nicely."

The police officer looked at me like I had just fallen off the turnip truck.

"That's not how this works, ma'am," he responded ever so curtly. "Now, before you make another move, why don't you tell me why you were reaching for your purse."

So, I explained the situation, but not before educating him on the differences between a purse and a pocketbook. I'm a natural-born teacher. Anyway, I told him that I had managed to get a snapshot of the license plate number with my phone and that I wanted to show him. He then reached into my pocketbook himself, which was more than a little embarrassing given the contents that I routinely carry around, and managed to pull my phone out. He handed it to me, and after unlocking the device, I pulled up the license plate picture to show him.

"Ma'am, this image is very blurry. I'm not sure it's of any use, to be honest. All this image does is corroborate your earlier statement that the car that hit yours was silver. Not much to go on."

"That's funny. It looks clear enough to me," I lied some more. "Want me to tell you what the letters and numbers are? Have you thought about having your eyes examined? Like, maybe you could benefit from a good pair of glasses. I know a wonderful optometrist here in town. I'd be happy to give you his name and number."

He started shaking his head in disbelief, and for a brief moment, I considered that I might have overstepped my bounds. But what else could I do? I didn't think it wise to let him know that I had had a little help clearing the image up from Chessy. I needed to convince him somehow that I could indeed read the letters and numbers of that license plate.

"Ma'am, I'd like you to give me your license and registration, and then I'd like for you to step out of the car."

"Is that really necessary?" I asked, starting to feel a bit anxious.

He nodded, so I obliged. I got permission to reach inside my pocketbook to retrieve my license and then took the registration out of the glove box. I handed both to the officer as I stepped out of my car in frustration. He asked me a couple of questions and then commanded me to walk in a straight line. I couldn't believe it. He thought I was drunk. He even went so far as to retrieve a Breathalyzer from his patrol car and insisted that I blow into the damned thing. When I passed all his stupid tests, he sighed in defeat. He was so sure I was drunk.

"Now, will you believe me when I tell you that I can read the letters and numbers on that image?" I asked, trying to rein in my anger.

He didn't know what else to do but to let me show him, so I went back to my car and retrieved my phone again. He took another long look at the blurry image before giving up and allowing me to proceed. I pointed to each letter and digit and showed him how I was able to identify them by looking at the pattern of the pixels once I zoomed in a bit, which was a version of the truth in my opinion. I told him what I had been able to determine and that there was only one number that I was still unsure of, but that it was either a five or a six.

"Ma'am, I'm not sure I believe any of what you have said, but I will run the plate number both ways and see what we come up with. Maybe one of these will come back as belonging to the silver car that allegedly hit you."

"Allegedly? You mean you still don't believe me?"

"I didn't say that. Those of us in law enforcement try not to jump to conclusions. You know, innocent until proven guilty."

That didn't make a whole lot of sense to me, since we weren't anywhere near a courtroom trial, but I let it go. I knew I was skating on thin ice with this officer and that one wrong word might land me behind bars or worse. He thought I was drunk moments ago, and if I became belligerent with him now, he could try to place me under psychiatric observation somewhere. I looked down at myself and realized I was still wearing my "Screw the Government" shirt from earlier. Damn. I should have thought to change clothes before trying to entrap a cop.

Anyway, I waited somewhat patiently while the police officer went back to his patrol car to run the license plate numbers. I could see through the windshield that he was talking to his partner, updating him on the current situation, while he worked his little computer to pull up the registrations. Judging by his facial expressions as he spoke to the other, I could tell he still had his doubts about me and my story. Then they both started laughing as he got out of the patrol car to make his way back over to where I was standing.

"Well?" I asked.

"Ma'am," he said, speaking louder than he needed to. "Must be your lucky day. One of the plates does match a silver car, a late model Mercedes."

"And to think, you had so little faith in me," I laughed.

"We'll file a report and investigate the owner of the car. We've already got your information, so there's nothing more that we need from you at this point in time. Are you all right to drive off on your own? Sometimes people who've been in accidents are a little too shaken up to get back behind the wheel right away. If you would like, I can drive you back home in your car, and my partner will follow behind us."

I had to admit, I wasn't so opposed to sitting next to this hunky police officer in my car for a while, maybe even "accidentally" cop a feel. But I didn't want him that badly, and I still had a mission to complete.

"Thank you, but no. I can drive myself. All I need now is the name of the person who owns that car, and I'll be on my way."

"Sorry, ma'am, but I can't give that information to you at this point in time. Once we've determined that the owner of the car was also driving it, and that the car was indeed the one that hit you, then we will have you both exchange information. We'll have to charge him for the hit-and-run as well. Our first step will be to locate the car and inspect it for damage that is consistent with the dents your car sustained."

"Not necessary. All I need is the name of the person, and I'll go investigate it myself. I don't want to press charges or anything." I said, probably too quickly.

"That decision, unfortunately, won't be up to you. If he committed a crime, we have to charge him. If he hit your car and then sped away, as you claimed, then he will be charged with a hit-and-run."

"But it was my car he hit. Shouldn't it be up to me?" I asked, getting desperate.

"No, ma'am."

"So you're not going to give me his name?" I asked one more time, feeling incredibly deflated.

"No, ma'am."

My plan was going up in flames. I had staged this whole damned thing just to get the guy's name, the name of the guy in that photograph with Scott. All I wanted was a simple name. Was that too much to ask for? Now what was I going to do? How was I going to get myself out of this mess? I couldn't very well tell the officer that I faked an accident, could I? If I did, he'd drag me down to the station, fingerprint me, take my mug shot, and throw me in the slammer. I looked up into his beautiful eyes and sighed.

"I'm not feeling well," I said as I tried my best at a fainting spell without actually fainting. "Perhaps I will take you up on your offer to drive me back to my place."

I figured even if the police do go inspect that silver car, they won't find any damage on it, and that'll be the end of it. With no other leads, they'll close the case. I really hated that I had to pretend to be "out of it" to extricate myself from this brilliant plan run amok. It was a real blow to my ego.

16

The hunky police officer dropped me back off at B-Block, parking my car about as far away from the entrance as he could. As he got into the patrol car his partner was driving, I began my slow walk of shame into the building. No, not that walk of shame. The walk of shame of a woman who thought she had so expertly planned her little escapade that she overlooked one key element. The law was not on her side, and she could not bend the law to her will.

As I entered the lobby of the building, I noticed out of the corner of my eye that Julie was staring at me very intently. I paid her no mind. I made my way to the elevator and pushed the button to go up, but before I knew it, Julie was by my side and invading my personal space. She needed a breath mint in the worst way, but as luck would have it, I didn't have one to give to her. Her continued staring was starting to creep me out a bit, but still, I tried to ignore her.

When the elevator finally opened, I stepped inside and pressed the button for my floor. All I wanted was to get up to my cell, take my clothes off, and sleep for about twenty-four hours. But Julie had other plans for me. She stepped inside the elevator after me and rode up to my floor in silence. I figured maybe she needed to check on another resident, so I paid her no mind.

As the doors opened on my floor, I stepped out, turned around to wave at Julie, and managed to smack her in the face in the process. I hadn't realized she had stepped out of the elevator behind me and, since she was again invading my personal space, my right hand accidentally made contact with her left cheek. I don't think I hit her hard, but it was quite a shock to the both of us. Her eyes opened wide, and she attempted to speak but she was in some sort of state of paralysis. She couldn't move.

I finally broke the silence by asking her what in the hell she was doing following me around at such a close distance. She didn't speak, so I turned around and walked toward the door to my cell. It took her a few seconds to move, but she caught up with me, and I asked her again why she was tailing me. This time, she spoke. She said that a police officer had called Springtime Pastures, and specifically B-Block, to let the staff know that they were bringing back one of their residents who seemed very confused and disoriented. The police officer suggested that the staff keep a very close eye on the resident, whom they named, in case she was going to need medical attention. The police officer apparently felt that I could be a danger to myself in my present condition.

So, that's what Julie was doing. She was keeping a very close eye on me. She took what the police officer said literally to a T, and I wasn't in the mood to explain to her what had actually happened. I tried to convince her that I was all right, but she said she had a duty to watch over me, and that's exactly what she was going to do, no matter how much I protested. So, I decided to make lemonade out of lemons and invited her in, figuring now was as good a time as any for the two of us to make an attempt at guessing the password to Scott's laptop.

After I ushered her into my cell, Julie took a seat on my sofa while I put away my keys and my pocketbook. I asked her if she wanted something nonalcoholic to drink, though I didn't have much to offer. When she asked for some sweet tea, I had to be the bearer of bad news. Not that I was particularly broken up about doing so, mind you. I wasn't exactly in a hospitable mood, given that she insisted on remaining in my presence until she was convinced that I was okay. I offered her a choice of water or diet soda. She chose the water, so I filled up a glass of the best tap water in the building and handed it to her, without ice.

To her credit, she took the glass of water graciously, and I fetched a diet soda for myself from the refrigerator. Grabbing Scott's laptop from the counter where I had laid it after returning from the library earlier, I took a seat next to Julie on the sofa. I explained to her that we might as well put our time to good use now, rather than wait until her shift was over for the day. She nodded in agreement and attempted to wrest the laptop from my grip. Oh, how she underestimated my strength. I was in the driver's seat on this one, and there was nothing she could do about it. It was my way or the highway, and I made sure she understood.

We started talking about Scott, his life, his interests, etc. Anything we could think of that might somehow lead us to the password we needed to gain access. Every combination of his birthdate, his address, his parents' names, his favorite pets, his college alma mater, everything! We came up empty. Then we started coming up with random passwords that we thought he might have used if he wasn't creative enough to come up with something unique. Like, Password 1234 or PassWord1234. Still no luck.

I asked Julie if there was anything of a more private nature that Scott might have confided to her, something that might have made a good password. Like, maybe if he preferred a particular sex position or perhaps a favorite sex toy or even a sexual fantasy. Okay, so maybe I wanted a little fantasy of my own in which I was somehow involved with one or more of the aforementioned possibilities with Scott. But I was running out of ideas and was willing to scrape the bottom of the barrel if that's what it took. Which surprised me, to be perfectly honest. I wasn't all that gung-ho about investigating his death in the first place, and now I was like a dog with a bone about it.

Feeling dejected, I leaned back on the sofa and let out a big sigh. Julie asked me if I was all right, panic starting to rise in her voice, but I assured her that nothing was wrong. Just one of the many inconveniences of living in an old-folks home. Anytime you emit even the slightest bodily noise, the staff gets all panicky, like you're about to keel over, leaving them with a mountain of paperwork to fill out should you expire on their watch. Heaven forbid!

Julie asked me if, perhaps, I'd like to order room service for dinner tonight so I wouldn't have to deal with the crowd downstairs in the dining room. I was tempted to, even if it meant having to eat a stone-cold meal. But the mention of dinner gave me an idea, and I rose from the sofa in search of that picture of Scott and that man in a dimly lit restaurant. I hadn't had much luck today, but I had a feeling my fortunes were about to turn around.

"Do you recognize this man sitting with Scott?" I asked Julie as I handed her the picture a moment later.

"No, I don't think so. He's handsome, though. I think I'd remember meeting him."

"Yes, my thoughts exactly," I added.

She asked me if I knew the man, which kind of annoyed me a bit. If I had known the man, I would have mentioned who he was before asking her. I'm not in the habit of playing games with people. Well, okay, so maybe I am in the habit of playing games with people, sometimes. But not tonight. I told her that, no, I didn't know who he was and was hoping that she did. I chose not to reveal the little episode I had with the man when I saw him at the library earlier today. I wasn't in the mood for a lecture from her about the dangers in confronting total strangers, even in public places.

I then asked Julie if she recognized the restaurant where Scott and the man were eating when this photo was taken. She said she didn't and added that she and Scott usually ordered delivery for dinner on the many nights they had spent together, so she wasn't really up to date on the restaurant scene in the area. And then she added for good measure that it was way more convenient because they didn't have to put on clothes just to eat a meal. Plus, they typically ordered two meals each since they usually worked up quite an appetite from their evening activities. Well, I wasn't interested in fantasizing about Julie and Scott together. I was interested in fantasizing about *me* and Scott together!

Taking the photo back from Julie, I decided to give it another once over before setting it aside in defeat. I scrutinized every detail of the scene, from the lighting to the décor and the food on the table. I realized something. Well, two things. First, Scott and this man weren't posing for the photo. Someone had taken it without their cooperation or, perhaps, even their knowledge. They were staring at each other, seemingly engaged in conversation, but their faces were angled at such a way that the camera was able to capture them pretty clearly. Instead of sitting opposite each other at the table, as I had previously thought, they were sitting *next* to each other.

The second thing I noticed was the suit Scott was wearing. Yes, the restaurant lighting was dim, but it wasn't so dark that I couldn't tell the color and style of the suit. And if I wasn't mistaken, he was wearing the same suit jacket I'd found that bizarre name and phone number in when Rebecca and I were scouring Scott's closet for clues. I stood and went to my nightstand to retrieve the piece of paper. Why I had placed it in my nightstand drawer I wasn't sure. If I were going to become a detective full time, I would have to come up with a better and more organized filing system.

"Does this name and number mean anything to you?" I asked Julie as I sat back down next to her with the paper in hand.

"I don't think so," she responded. "Does it mean anything to you?"

I told her that it didn't, and this time I also told her that I wouldn't have asked if I had already known who or what "Cardinal" referred to. She nodded but seemed not to notice my increasing frustration with her. I told her that I had searched the number online but came up empty. She asked if I had tried to call the number, but I told her that I hadn't. I'm not sure why I hadn't. Maybe because I had no reason to believe, up until now, that this piece of paper could possibly have any relevance to Scott's death.

Julie took her phone out of her pocket, grabbed the paper out of my hand, and dialed the number. A few rings later, an automated message came through saying that the number was no longer in service. Damn. I felt like I was hitting a series of dead ends. Clues that went nowhere. Maybe not even clues at all. More like desperate attempts to make sense out of the death of a healthy young man who should still have had the majority of his life to live.

But this man Scott was having dinner with in that photo—he meant something. He had to have meant something to Scott.

Enough for Scott to keep the photo, and yet not enough to actually place the photo on a page in the album. And if I was right about the suit whose pocket held the name and number I'd found and the suit Scott was wearing in the photo being one and the same, then I had to be on to something. Even if it wasn't related to Scott's death, there was some meaning here. Something important to Scott's life.

Acting on a hunch, I took the piece of paper back from Julie, opened the laptop, and started testing various combinations of the name *Cardinal* and the phone number listed below, feeling a renewed sense of hope that I might have found the password. I tried all sorts of combinations: capitalizing the first letter, leaving off the 1 before the area code, typing the phone number with dashes and then without, and capitalizing the entire name. I was about to give up when, finally, I hit paydirt. I typed it exactly as it appeared on the paper, but included an underscore between Cardinal and the phone number, and voila! The laptop accepted the password.

I was so excited to have finally achieved a win that I loosened my grip enough to allow Julie to seize the laptop from me. She said she wanted to search for those porn videos and delete them before we proceeded any further. I told her there was no way in hell I was going to miss the opportunity to see a full-frontal Scott. I would allow her to delete those videos only after I inspected them very closely for myself. No detail would be left unnoticed. No matter how small or big.

Julie didn't budge. I tried to grab the laptop back from her, but she resisted, moving the laptop out of my reach. I told her I wasn't in the mood to play this particular game and demanded she relinquish the laptop. It wasn't just about the porn videos. I was afraid she might accidentally delete something else. Something of some significance relating to Scott's death. Or at least Scott's life leading up to his death. If she didn't want me to see the porn videos, fine. I was half joking about them anyway. But she was not going to delete a single file off that laptop without my say-so.

I waited for a moment to give Julie time to reassess her current situation, and when that moment was up, I threw her a curveball. I reminded her that I had caught her pilfering supplies from the on-site beauty salon and that I had heard rumors of other, possibly shady dealings she'd had with some of the residents. I was willing to bet that Chessy wasn't the only resident that she had been "helping" with procuring items they weren't supposed to have. If I was wrong, I had to hope Chessy would forgive me for spilling her beans. But I was also betting that Julie would relent rather than call my bluff, since I had no intention of actually reporting her to the administration here. I admired her entrepreneurial attitude. Truly, I did.

When I made it clear that I wasn't backing down, she relented and handed me the laptop. I promised her that if we came across those porn videos, I would regretfully allow her to delete them. And with that settled, we were ready to begin.

17

It took Julie and me a while to figure out how to navigate around Scott's laptop. He had one of those Apple computers, and neither Julie nor I had had much experience using one. We did eventually find where the bulk of his files were located, and as we started scanning through them, we began to wonder how well either of us ever really knew him. Sure, we found the porn videos Julie was so worried about, and after I "accidentally" opened one or two of them, I allowed her to delete all of them in bulk. Fortunately, he had used Julie's name as part of the filenames for all the videos she was featured in.

The problem was, there were a ton of other videos to go through. Some featured Scott solo sitting in front of a camera talking about various topics, from politics and religion to sports, interior decoration, personal hygiene products, and his love of the outdoors. Maybe he had a YouTube channel I wasn't aware of? But sandwiched between these various videos were other videos that he had clearly taken but in which he didn't appear. A number of videos featured people who were going about their daily lives in complete ignorance of the fact that they were being filmed. Some featured various people of noteworthy fame giving speeches. There was a video Scott must have taken at a political rally with our governor, for example.

But one video in particular caught our attention. A video featuring a man talking into the camera, having a conversation with Scott who wasn't in the picture. I recognized the man immediately as the same man from the photo. He looked younger, though, maybe about ten years younger than he appeared in person at the library earlier. They were talking pretty casually at first, but then Scott started asking questions about the man's work. Turned out, the man had recently launched a company called Cardinal Construction. Well, now we knew where the Cardinal name came from.

One problem with the interview, however, was that there was no introduction, or perhaps the introduction had been sliced off. So, we had no name for the man. At least not yet. I wasn't sure why Scott had interviewed this man to begin with. Did they know each other back then? Was Scott trying to start a career as a journalist? If I'm right about the age of this video, then Scott was still swimming competitively for a living. Perhaps, he knew his days as a professional swimmer were numbered and was attempting to sow the seeds of his second act.

What bothered me more, though, was the way this Cardinal man was looking into the camera. I didn't know for sure where Scott was sitting in relation to the man while he was interviewing him. But I was betting good money that he was somewhere behind the camera, very much in the man's line of sight. The man was simply glowing, almost to the point of actually flirting with Scott. I looked over at Julie to see if she was picking up on this, but she wasn't. She was bored. But here was this man, who had a daughter and a wife, positively beaming at Scott.

Fortunately, Julie's cell phone rang. She answered the call and promptly got up from her seat. She said she had to leave to take care of an emergency downstairs, involving a resident who was performing a striptease in the lobby. I just hoped it wasn't Chessy playing up her dementia act again. I had tried to tell her she needed to tone things down a bit, like maybe going easy on the sequins, but she was her own woman and was going to do things her way, even if she did end up landing herself in a memory care facility as a result.

Anyway, I told Julie I'd keep sifting through the videos while she was gone. She told me she thought I'd better wait for her return before continuing our investigation and made a move to snatch the laptop back from me again. But I was too quick for her this time.

"I'm perfectly capable of doing this by myself," I stated as her hands narrowly missed the bottom of the laptop. "Don't worry, I'll fill you in on what else I discover."

She began to complain, saying that she wasn't moving from her spot until I handed it over to her, but I reminded her of the resident down below who was probably pretty close to full nakedness by now. It worked, and Julie reluctantly left my cell.

I started thinking more about this man, this Cardinal man. He was smitten with Scott. Anyone with eyes, ears, or even half a functioning brain would have come to the same conclusion. Except Julie, of course. So the only question I had left now was whether the situation had worked in reverse as well. At the very least, Scott had maintained some level of contact with Mr. Cardinal for a number of years. Plus, he used "Cardinal" and that phone number as his password for his laptop.

Despite the recurrence of Mr. Cardinal in the picture, at the library, and now in this video, however, I still had no proof that he had anything to do with Scott's death other than a gnawing hunch that wouldn't let go. I called Anna Lee to give her an update and asked her to convene the other women at her house to discuss what I had learned thus far. I wasn't sure about giving all the details over the phone, since I didn't know how she would initially react if I suggested Scott and this man might have had some sort of relationship. You never can tell with these elderly southern belles. She might be like "well, whatever made him happy…it's none of my business." Or her reaction might be more along the lines of "he couldn't have been a homosexual. He was my water aerobics instructor, after all." Like that would have made any sense. Better to lay this theory out in a group setting so I'd have some backup from Rebecca if needed.

Anyway, Anna Lee asked me if I'd be up for having dinner at her place this evening, assuming she could also get the other women to attend. I wasn't, but I pretended otherwise and gladly accepted her invitation. She called back a few moments later to let me know that Lanie was unavailable for dinner tonight, but that they were all free for lunch tomorrow. She said she'd have her domestic helper fix some sandwiches for us and asked me if I had a preference, which I didn't. I thanked her and said I'd see her tomorrow at lunchtime.

Having a few moments to kill before going downstairs for dinner and not knowing what else to do, I sat back on the sofa and turned on the TV. I flipped through the limited number of channels available here and landed on one of the local stations airing a soap opera episode. I wasn't a regular soap opera viewer by any stretch of the imagination, but once in a while, I'd catch an episode here or there, not really knowing what was going on but finding myself enthralled nonetheless.

The scene I stumbled into involved a woman and her identical twin sister confronting the man they both had been sleeping with, unbeknownst to each other. The man tried to play it off casually, stating that he thought they were one and the same but used different names on different days. Or something like that. Well, as identical as they might have been, even I knew that there were ways to tell the difference and that this shlub of a man either hadn't bothered to notice or was more likely having the time of his life double dipping into that particular gene pool.

I was really getting into this episode when the local news station interrupted with a breaking news report. Damn. I was looking forward to a fight, the twins taking turns smacking the man upside the head with their purses or worse. I was about to change the channel, but for reasons I still can't fully explain, I didn't and settled in to listen to what the news folks were about to report.

"This is a breaking news bulletin from your most trusted source for local news. We're coming to you live from the capitol here in Raleigh where a seismic shift in the balance of power of our state government is about to occur. Sources confirm that Wake County Representative Alicia Lassiter, currently a Democratic representative from the Cary area, has decided to switch parties and become a Republican. No information has been given at this point in time regarding her reasons for switching parties," the newscaster said.

Breaking news? Really? This was worth interrupting an unusually interesting soap opera episode? Now, if they had come on the air and said that recreational marijuana was being legalized in North Carolina, that would have been breaking news worth watching. If they had come on the air and said that all daughters had a legal obligation to house their homeless mothers in their own homes, that would have been breaking news worth watching. If they had come on the air and said that all men of a certain age were going to have to start plucking their nose hairs, that would have been breaking news worth watching. But this? No. Like I said before, I never cared much for politics, and neither party had ever done much for me as far as I could tell.

"The results of last fall's elections here in North Carolina were very favorable to the Republicans. They flipped the state supreme court, won all the court of appeals races, won the US Senate race, and did very well in the legislative races. They regained a veto-proof supermajority in the state senate, which they had lost four years earlier, and they came one vote shy of having a similar supermajority in the state house. With Representative Lassiter's anticipated switch, they will now have that supermajority in the house as well. This means that the Republicans in both chambers in the state legislature now have the ability to override the Democratic governor's vetoes completely on their own."

So what, I thought. I've lived long enough now to see both parties have veto proof majorities at one time or another. They were acting like the tectonic plates underneath us were about to shift in ways that would reverberate for years. Well, I'm sixty-seven years old, and not once in my lifetime has marijuana ever been legalized here. Not once in my sixty-seven years has the legislature ever really given two shits about its constituents. It's always been about money and power. I didn't see that changing anytime soon just because one legislator was about to switch parties, even if her switch handed her new party a supermajority.

"A number of hot-button issues from abortion and birth control to gun laws and school vouchers are about to take on new significance as the anticipated new supermajority in the state house begins to flex its muscles along with its counterpart in the state senate. Over the last four years, with Republicans in control of the legislature but without a supermajority and a Democrat in the governor's mansion, the State of North Carolina has avoided, for better or worse, dealing with many of these issues because the two sides are miles apart from each other. That changes now, as we're about to see the balance of power shift decisively to the right once Representative Lassiter makes her party switch official."

I had to admit one thing was bothering me about this news. I've always been a "what you see is what you get" kind of person. I know I'm a little on the eccentric side, but it's who I truly am, and I wouldn't want to pretend to be something or someone I wasn't. Never really having thought much about party switchers before, I was starting to think about them now. I didn't have much faith in our electoral system, but what about those who did?

"We're getting word that Representative Lassiter will be giving a press conference to announce the change of her party affiliation, but we do not have a timetable for that yet. Our sources are now telling us that the legislative staff is in the process of moving her desk from the Democratic side to the Republican side as we speak. Of course, we will have full coverage of this event as it continues to unfold, with interviews from leaders of both parties on their take regarding Representative Lassiter's reasons for switching."

I took out my phone and googled her, since I frankly didn't even know what she looked like. I quickly discovered that she was actually my state representative. I probably should have known that, but I didn't. I'm one of those very occasional voters who vote only for the top races in any given year. I couldn't tell you who her opponent was or whether I even voted in that particular race. You know how those ballots are. So many races. So many names. It's hard to keep track of who's who! And unless a candidate is getting up on TV with ads, I'm not very likely to have a clue about what their stances are on the issues.

But when I looked Ms. Lassiter up, I was pretty surprised at what I found when I stumbled upon her campaign website from the previous election. The issues she claimed to support would have made Rebecca's heart swoon and Lanie's stomach churn. She had indeed presented herself as a true-blue Dem, and that is how she managed to win her election here on the west side of the county. This area was once pretty reliably red, but population migration from out of state brought a blue tidal wave with it.

I wondered what could have made her switch less than a year after winning that election. Seemed like such a coincidence to me, especially given the rhetoric I was reading on her campaign site. She didn't just support the standard causes of the Democratic party. She was practically militant about her support, talking about how this group was under attack and that group was under attack and everyone's rights were under attack. She promoted herself as a warrior for the left and a voice for the unheard and underrepresented.

Navigating to the next page on her site, I found a list of endorsements, none of which was surprising based on who she was claiming to be. Several environmental groups, several women's reproductive health groups, one of the LGBTQ groups based here in North Carolina, and a slew of others. There were videos, too, of her stump speech and of other campaign events where she was interacting with her potential constituents, answering their questions about the issues most important to them. But did she mean any of what she said or was she simply trying to get votes? I've always subscribed to the philosophy that you should mean what you say and say what you mean. Perhaps Ms. Lassiter simply felt differently.

I found one more video on another page, her biography page, in which she talked about her life leading up to the moment that she initiated her campaign. And finally, she brought her husband and daughter into the video to introduce them to the world, and my jaw just about dropped to the floor. Her husband and the man I had been chasing after were one and the same. I was absolutely sure of it.

18

"Yes, I'm positive," I said to the other ladies as we ate our lunch at Anna Lee's the next day. "It's him. It's definitely him."

"Well, my word," Anna Lee responded. "I have to admit I'm having a hard time believing that our Scotty would have knowingly associated himself with such a man."

"And what do you mean by that?" Rebecca asked. "That Scott might have had a relationship of some sort with another man, or that he had somehow managed to befriend the husband of a politician?"

"No, whatever you might think of me, I am not a prude," Anna Lee responded. "Just because I talk in a slower, more melodic tone than you brash northerners do doesn't mean I'm stupid. Or ignorant. What I'm talking about is that failed construction business of his. It was all over the news last year during the election. He was accused of embezzling money from his own company. Got off on a technicality if I remember correctly. Somehow, his wife managed to avoid scrutiny and won her election."

"And now she's switched parties," I explained."

"Yes, you already said that," Lanie chimed in. "Sounds like she made a wise choice to me! She'll be much happier as a Republican anyway. Republicans are much more likely to lead happy, fulfilling lives. It's a proven fact! If you don't believe me, look at mine. Couldn't be happier. Everything came up roses for me! Perfect husband. Perfect children."

"And perfect breasts," I laughed. "Don't forget the perfect breasts! Filled with silicone, though they might be."

"So what? What God didn't give me, my rich husband provided. There's nothing wrong with spending a little money on your looks if it makes you happy."

She realized her mistake a moment too late. Never before had she ever admitted to having breast augmentation surgery. The cat's out of the bag now!

"Anyway," I said, "we don't have any proof that Mr. Lassiter was involved with Scott's death, but when Rebecca and I cornered him at the library, he visibly flinched. Whether it was because he thought he was about to be accused of having an affair in front of his daughter or because he already knew of Scott's death and wanted to avoid any appearance of culpability or involvement remains a question we have to answer. It may lead us to a dead end, but we have to know for sure before looking at other suspects. Especially since we have no other leads to go on at the moment."

The other ladies nodded in agreement, Lanie begrudgingly so. But the most pressing question on my mind was how? With his wife's party switch, I had a feeling he was going to be very difficult to pin down in any sort of public setting. She ended up not giving that press conference the news anchor had promised, and I was betting he was lying low as well. At least until the political storm blew over. They say a year in politics is a lifetime, and Mr. and Mrs. Lassiter were about to test that adage. How long would it take for everyone to forget she even switched parties in the first place?

"So, where do we start?" Rebecca asked.

"If we were back in my home state of Alabama," Anna Lee said, "I could have leveraged my connections in Montgomery. I was on a first-name basis with many of the political power brokers on both sides of the aisle there. I'd have been able to dig up whatever skeletons had been buried."

"But you're not in Alabama anymore," Lanie reminded her.

"I'm not demented, Lanie," Anna Lee replied. "I know exactly where I am, and I know exactly who I can impose upon to help get us access to those who might be able to shed some light on the Lassiters."

"Who?" Lanie asked.

"Why, you, of course, dear," Anna Lee said, barely concealing her surprise that Lanie was playing coy.

"What can I do? I don't know the Lassiters personally," Lanie responded.

"No, dear, I figured not, since they were until very recently members of the opposing party. But on more than one occasion, you have regaled us with stories of your connections to various people in politically powerful positions within the Republican Party in the county and in the capitol. Why, Raleigh is a stone's throw from our little community here at Springtime Pastures."

"I'm still not following," Lanie insisted.

"What I am trying to say, dear, is that if our poor Scotty was, indeed, involved in some way with Mr. Lassiter, whether romantically or some other means we do not yet know, wouldn't you expect the Republicans to want to know about any such issues before agreeing to let his wife join their caucus? Don't you think they would have insisted on knowing about any potentially embarrassing circumstances that might come to light? Like, knowing where all the land mines are buried before you walk onto a battlefield."

Lanie's eyes bugged out of her head.

"So, what exactly do you want me to do?" she asked.

Anna Lee looked at me for help, figuring that I was likely to be able to formulate a plan more quickly than she could. Ever the queen that she was, she had a particular knack for delegating tasks she either couldn't or didn't want to do herself. And I had to admit that there was something to that old phrase about staying in one's lane. She was right. Craftiness wasn't her forte. It was mine. Which was probably why I was here in the first place.

"Okay," I said as I turned my gaze back toward Lanie. "Let's start by making a list of all the politicians you know at the legislature. The higher up they are in the pecking order the better, but we'll go with what you've got."

Anna Lee rang for her domestic helper and asked the helper to bring back a pad and a pen.

"You can't be serious. Do you just expect me to go up to them and ask if they know anything about Mr. Lassiter and an ex-Olympic swimmer who recently died?" Lanie asked.

"No, of course not. I mean, that's probably what I would do, but I'm not you," I responded as a smile broadened across my face.

Lanie asked me why I was smiling, but I didn't care. I had figured out how we were going to start getting some answers.

"You're going to throw a party," I stated.

"Excuse me?' Lanie asked. "Setting aside the fact that I have no idea where you're going with this, I think it's very presumptuous of you to even suggest that I throw a party. Do you know how much effort goes into throwing a successful party? No, of course you don't. Look at you. Your idea of a successful party is a bag of weed and enough bongs to go around. And maybe a designated area for the pile of underwear!"

"Well, first, let me say that I'm pleasantly surprised you know what a bong is. I wouldn't have expected that of you. Then again, you've had one shoved up your rear end ever since I've known you, so I guess I shouldn't have been that surprised. And for your information, I did help my daughter plan her wedding, so I do know a thing or two about throwing a respectable party without the presence of herbal supplements or, for that matter, group sex."

"Ladies," Anna Lee interjected, "let's remember that we're all on the same side here. We all want to find out what happened to our poor, dear Scotty."

Rebecca corrected Anna Lee, stating that we all knew what had happened to Scott but that we wanted to know whether foul play was involved and, if so, who and why. I glanced at Rebecca, giving her a "was that really necessary?" expression. She got the hint and closed her mouth.

"Listen," I said to Lanie, "you don't like me, and I don't much like you. I think, at the very least, we can agree on that. But Anna Lee is right. We're on the same side here. We all cared about Scott. Some maybe more than others. But still. We all want to find out how he died and why he died. And if someone in particular is responsible for his death, we want to know who. As I said before, we don't have any other leads right now, so we're going with what we've got. And what we've got is a party switcher whose husband had some sort of a relationship with Scott. Maybe a romantic relationship. Maybe a business relationship. Or maybe nothing more than a platonic friendship for all we know. But I'm telling you this,

Mr. Lassiter visibly flinched when I showed him Scott's picture yesterday. He knows something that we don't. Whatever that is, we need to find out."

"Well, I suppose I can agree to that. But I don't understand what throwing a party has to do with this."

Lanie looked at the other ladies, hoping for some help, but they were just as clueless as she was regarding my little plan. I had to revel in the moment. One true socialite, one wannabe socialite, and one retired Ivy League professor were all a step behind me. This is what happens when you spend your entire life in a country club, begging to get into a country club, or stuffed away in an ivory tower full of other learned people with no street smarts.

"Think about it for a moment. Alicia Lassiter has switched parties. She currently represents a blue area, and even if the legislature finds some way to redraw her district before her next election, she's going to have a tough fight ahead of her. This area is too blue for a Republican to win without putting in a whole lot of effort and a whole lot of money."

Rebecca asked me how I knew so much about politics and elections when I had never given off the impression that I cared for the subject in the slightest. I told her that you don't have to care about a subject to know about it. I asked her how many of her former colleagues still cared about the subjects they taught after years of sitting in those secure and comfortable tenured chairs. She conceded the point.

"Well," Lanie said, "I'll definitely be donating to her next campaign for sure!"

"That's lovely of you," I responded, "but one maxed-out contribution won't be enough, and I'm betting Mrs. Lassiter knows that. She's going to need a lot of money, and she's going to need it soon. She'll have to get through a Republican primary first, and even though she'll probably have the backing of the leadership in the legislature, questions will swirl around her regarding where her true loyalties lie. If she can switch parties once, she can do it again. And I'm betting there are enough voters on your side of the aisle who'll be somewhat suspect of her. Enough so that another Republican could easily primary her."

"They wouldn't dare," Lanie said in all sincerity.

"Of course, they would," I answered.

"Millie's right," Rebecca chimed in. "I would be very suspect of a Republican changing parties all of a sudden. At the very least, I'd want to know more about why before supporting them as a Democrat."

"See?" I added. "So, now that we've established that Mrs. Lassiter is going to need a lot of money, we have an opening."

I looked around the room to see if anyone was starting to pick up on what I was getting at. No luck.

"Okay, so one of the quickest ways to get a lot of money is to hold a fundraiser event. Hence, the party."

All the light bulbs in the room turned on at once.

"But," Anna Lee said, "those types of events can take a long, long time to plan. There are so many considerations that have to be taken into account. I haven't ever hosted a political fundraiser, but back in the day, I served on several charitable boards and was very involved in the planning and execution of their annual fundraising events."

"This doesn't need to be that big," I responded. "We just need, say, forty to fifty guests, a headliner, a venue, and a caterer. Maybe charge $5,000 a plate or whatever we think we can get away with."

"Sounds like you've got this all figured out," Lanie said, looking at me, "so why should I get involved?"

"Because you're the one with the connections. You're the only one of the four of us who could credibly pull this off. And by pulling this off, I mean getting wealthy Republican butts in those seats. Oh, and I figure you can front the money for the venue and catering."

Anna Lee looked at me with a new sense of admiration. Not that I needed her approval to bolster my own self-worth, but I was appreciative, nonetheless. Rebecca looked at me skeptically, though, perhaps unsure whether this plan was going to work.

"While you're playing the role of hostess at the event, the rest of us will discreetly strike up conversations with those present and steer those conversations as delicately as we can to the subject at hand. Namely, getting as much information on Mr. Lassiter as possible, along with whatever tidbits we can find out about their marriage. We'll get them good and liquored up and then gently prompt them to reveal what they know."

"There's one big problem with your plan," Rebecca said. "Mr. Lassiter has already seen both of us. If he's at this fundraiser, he'll surely recognize us. You're a pretty unforgettable woman, Millie, and I'm sure he saw me chasing after his car, trying to get a picture of his license plate number. If he's there, he'll recognize us in an instant."

I was about to respond to Rebecca when Anna Lee chimed in. She offered to spring for a complete makeover for both of us. She said by the time the stylist had worked her magic, we'd be unrecognizable. I wasn't sure if she meant that to be a compliment or a criticism, but her idea certainly got me thinking. Sure, we could change our looks, but what about our voices, specifically mine, since Mr. Lassiter had heard me speak? Anna Lee suggested that I keep any speaking to a minimum. When I wasn't satisfied with her suggestion, she proposed hiring a voice coach to help me alter my pitch and my accent. She said it'd be an improvement. Now I know that wasn't a compliment. That was almost a "bless your heart" moment.

"You know," Lanie said, "I still haven't agreed to be a part of this, let alone act as hostess."

"What part of this plan gave you the impression that you had a choice?" Rebecca asked her. "It's three against one. So unless you want me to spread around to the entire community that your knockers are fake, you'll do what we tell you to do."

Lanie conceded the point and agreed to the plan. We all figured finding a caterer to do the event wouldn't be too difficult, but we had to find a venue and find one quickly. We also had to set a date for this fundraiser, which meant that someone was going to have to reach out to Mrs. Lassiter directly. I thought about the ethical implications of using a fundraiser to pump its attendees for information while also technically benefiting the party-switching guest of honor financially. Then I thought about poor Scott lying face down in the pool, and I abandoned any worry I had over such issues.

19

The four of us met again the following day for lunch to begin planning for the fundraiser. Lanie said she had already reached out to Mrs. Lassiter to see if she'd be interested in attending this fundraiser for her. Well, of course, she said yes. I was surprised Lanie was able to get through to her so quickly, but Lanie wasn't exaggerating when she said she had connections. She really had connections. She had even gotten Mrs. Lassiter to agree on a couple of possible dates, all within the next couple of weeks.

Anna Lee and Rebecca started talking about finding a suitable venue for the fundraiser, and while they appreciated my suggestion of having it at one of those places where the servers wear skimpy outfits to entice the men, they said they'd take care of the arrangements. I did suggest that they at least find some place with a kitchen that would offer full service so we wouldn't have to find a separate caterer.

I then had one of those divine moments in which a brilliant idea just pops into my head. I suggested they check out a country club I went to once years ago for an animal shelter fundraiser banquet. I couldn't quite remember the name of it, but I knew where it was, and once I described its location, Lanie knew exactly where I was talking about. Turns out she was a member of the club. So, Anna Lee and Rebecca were off the hook, sort of. Lanie still had to inquire about the availability of one of the dining rooms there, but she seemed confident that she'd be able to swing it somehow.

One detail we still hadn't managed to figure out was who we were going to get to emcee the event. Lanie would serve as the hostess, and I was sure Mrs. Lassiter herself would want to speak, but we needed a bigger name. Someone who would draw those wealthy Republicans in positions of power to come. Lanie was on a first-name basis with the speaker of the house, but I wasn't so sure he'd be enough. Oh, I wanted him in attendance, not that I knew who he was. But not as the headliner.

I asked Lanie if, perhaps, she had any contacts within the offices of either of our US Senators, both of whom were also Republican. She said she didn't. I asked Anna Lee if she still had any contacts within the offices of her home-state senators who could then act as liaisons to ours. She said she didn't. I then asked Rebecca if she had ever even spoken to a Republican politician in her entire life. She said she hadn't. I pointed out to her that maybe she should give it a try sometime. I suggested that most Democrats and Republicans aren't really all that different. Everyone cares about the same issues—

having food on the table, a roof over their heads, and clothes on their backs. Rebecca and Lanie both looked at me like I had lost my mind.

Oh, well. We were back to square one. No senators and no other politicians of a certain stature that any of us had any connection to. No one who owed us any favors. No one we could think of who we could conceivably get on such short notice. Lanie brought up the speaker again, and again I shot her down. She wasn't pleased.

After we had finished our lunch, I went back to B-Block, feeling at least somewhat hopeful, given that we had made a bit of progress on our plans. But we really needed to find a headliner. If we couldn't, I wasn't sure we'd be able to get Mrs. Lassiter to attend herself, let alone any of the power brokers within the Republican party. I thought about running all of this by Julie to see if she might have any connections, but I wasn't ready to tell her about our plans because doing so would necessitate revealing our suspicions about Scott and Mr. Lassiter. I didn't want to upset her in her delicate condition.

I was heading toward the elevator, which would take me up to my cell, when I heard the faint sound of someone singing. Well, curiosity got the better of me, and I followed the sound of the voice until I found its source. I entered the social hall to find a bedazzled Chessy doing what appeared to be a one-woman revival of *Sweeney Todd*, my favorite Stephen Sondheim musical. She was pitch perfect in her rendition of "A Little Priest," and I had to laugh when she sang the part about politicians being so oily that they're served with a doily. *How prescient*, I thought.

A couple of the other residents were sitting in chairs, enjoying the performance, but the room wasn't anywhere near capacity. Perhaps if the performance had made it onto the official schedule for the day's social activities, more would have shown up for it. Chessy was proving to be an outstanding singer. I started wondering whether her performance was too good, as in how could a dementia patient be singing so well and be remembering all the lyrics to these songs. But I remembered reading an article not long ago about the therapeutic effect of music for Alzheimer's patients and how patients who seemed so far gone would start singing the words to tunes they knew once the music started. So, maybe Chessy's performance wouldn't raise too much suspicion among the staff.

When she finally finished "A Little Priest," it's a long song by the way, she saw me standing in the corner of the room and beckoned me over. Chessy tried to convince me to sing another song from the musical with her as a duet, but I declined. I had many talents to be proud of, but singing wasn't one of them. I was completely tone deaf, and after many a critic told me so to my face, I knew it was true. When it's one person, you can pretty much chalk it up to bad taste, poor hearing, or just being overly critical. But when ten talent agents you approach to represent you when you're trying to become a breakout singer all tell you that you can't sing worth a damn, well, there's no point in continuing to pretend otherwise.

I asked Chessy if she thought she could take a little break from her set so I could speak with her about the latest developments in the investigation into Scott's death. She said she didn't want to disappoint her many adoring fans and made a big production out of it, too, waving her arms around the entire room as if she were singing to thousands of people in a packed stadium. I knew this was part of her dementia act, given that there were only three other residents in the room besides the two of us, so I said I'd wait for her to finish. I then took a seat at one of the nearby tables and sat back for the rest of the show.

Four songs later and with a seventy-five percent reduction in her audience, leaving me as the sole attendee, Chessy ended her performance. "A triumph," she called her finale, as she gazed adoringly at the nonexistent fans.

"Chessy," I said, "you can give up the act. No one else is in here; it's only you and me."

"Oh, thank God!" she exclaimed. "I'm pooped. Acting like I've got dementia is exhausting!"

"As they say, fake it 'til you make it," I laughed.

"That's one show I hope doesn't turn into reality," she said. "Anyway, tell me what progress you've made in your investigation."

So, I filled her in on my little escapade trying to coerce law enforcement into cooperating in the investigation, finally gaining access to the laptop, and then discovering the true identity of the man who kept showing up throughout all of this. I then explained the fundraiser plan that the other ladies and I had started working on to get some intel on Mr. Lassiter.

"But you still don't know if Mr. Lassiter had anything to do with Scott's death," Chessy pointed out.

"Well, no, but we don't have any other leads, so we're going with what we've got. You don't, by any chance, have connections with any influential Republicans, do you?"

"Afraid not. At least not anymore. I burned that bridge when I testified against one years ago who was involved in a bribery scandal. I became a persona non grata in Republican circles after that. Of course, this was twenty years ago now. But politicians aren't known for their forgiving attitudes. I doubt any of the Republicans I knew back then who are still in office today would speak to me if I tried reaching out."

"I understand, but let me ask you this. Would you be willing to attend this little fundraiser of ours? I have a feeling your forensic psychologist skills could really come in handy. You could help us determine who's being truthful and who's concealing the truth."

"Wish I could, but I'm not allowed to leave the premises. You know, the whole dementia act."

"Oh, right. I forgot. But maybe there's a way. Julie knows you're sane. Between the two of us, I'm sure we can come up with a strategy to, um, get Julie to look the other way when we leave. You could even provide some entertainment at the fundraiser. You know, you have a beautiful singing voice. We could come up with a backstory for you. Tell everyone you replaced Angela Lansbury in the original production of *Sweeney Todd* or something like that. We'd still need an actual politician of stature to headline the event, but you'd get second billing!"

"Now that sounds like fun. I could do a Sondheim review! Pick the best of the best of his songs."

"Yes, but maybe plan on limiting it to two or three. And pick songs that have some relation to the event's theme, if you can."

"Which is what?"

"Pumping rich Republicans for cash! I mean, we're secretly going to be pumping them for information. We're looking for anything they can discreetly tell us about Mr. Lassiter. But as far as they're concerned, we're providing them an opportunity to support the newest member of their party and, hopefully, to hear from an influential member from within their own ranks. Plus, a good meal, of course, and plenty of booze. What could be more wholesome than that?"

"Count me in!"

Now it's gonna be a real party, I thought as I left Chessy reveling in her plans to wow the audience. I just needed to make sure to remember to tell her to wear red, not purple, and certainly not blue. I didn't want anyone there getting suspicious and accusing her of being a spy or something. *Damn*, I realized I was going to have to get a new outfit as well. That navy blue suit I had, the only thing I had to wear that was nice enough for the fundraiser, wouldn't do. Well, I thought I could go to Goodwill and see what I could find in some sort of red hue on my limited budget.

After returning to my cell, I took a nap for an hour or two, dreams of the fundraiser floating in and out of my subconscious. I woke up to my cell phone ringing, quickly looked at the caller ID, debated whether to answer, and then resigned myself to accepting the call.

"Hello, Lanie," I said. "You just interrupted a very sexually satisfying dream I was having, so this better be good."

"I, um, well, sorry about that," she stammered, taken aback by my bluntness. "But I wanted to let you know that I reserved one of the dining rooms at the club and then reconfirmed with Representative Lassiter that she can make it on that evening. The dining room should seat fifty people comfortably, and there's a small movable stage that the club staff can move in there if we need one. Plus, they'll handle the sound equipment. You know, mics, speakers, etc."

"Wonderful!" I said as I shrugged the sleepiness off. "Umm, do you know if they by any chance have a karaoke machine?"

"Karaoke? Why? Planning on singing a song or two?" Lanie asked.

"Oh no, but I have a lead on some terrific entertainment, and she might need some musical backup. She's a Broadway legend and a close personal friend," I exaggerated.

"Oh, who? Is it Patti LuPone? Or maybe Bernadette Peters? I love them!"

"Don't I wish?" I laughed, thinking that neither was likely to agree to sing at a GOP event. "No, this person prefers to live a quieter life these days, so you might not remember her from back in the day. But she took over some very famous roles when the original actors moved along to other projects. I'll fill you in once I've confirmed her attendance."

"Keep me posted! I'll start working on the guest list. We'll have to do some advertising, of course, but I know enough politicians and other influential Republicans to fill at least half the seats!"

"Yes, we're counting on that! Fifty seats are a lot to fill on such short notice. Even if we do manage to land an A-list speaker. I know you have your heart set on the speaker of the house, but let's pencil him in as a backup. Sound good?"

"Sure, he owes me a favor anyway, so when I tell him to jump, all he'll do is ask me how high."

Lanie was positively giddy by the time we ended the call. You'd have thought I was her new best friend or something. She was losing sight of the intended purpose of this fundraiser, but I wasn't about to bring her back down to reality. I much preferred this Lanie to the one who was accusing me of murdering Scott a few days ago. I supposed there really was something to that old saying about politics making strange bedfellows.

Taking a seat on the sofa, I turned on the TV to catch another episode of that soap opera I tried to watch the other day. Five minutes into it, there was another "breaking news" interruption. I nearly threw the remote at the screen. How dare they interrupt yet another episode of my favorite soap! Okay, so I don't watch it that often, but still, when I'm in the mood for an episode, I want to actually watch one!

"We interrupt your regularly scheduled programming," the newscaster began, "to bring you this special report. Our sources have confirmed that the North Carolina Commissioner of Insurance, Republican Bradley Williams, plans to run for governor in next year's gubernatorial election. Since the current Democratic governor, Constance Elliot, is term-limited, this race is wide open, and Williams has officially thrown his hat in the ring."

This was hardly breaking news. The race was well over a year away at this point. I was sure a number of people would be jumping into the contest from both sides of the aisle before all was said and done. But then the image on the TV faded from the newsroom to a full-screen shot of the commissioner, and my heart suddenly skipped a beat. Sure, he was a lot older than when I last saw him, but I'd recognize those eyes anywhere. Those same eyes peered at me with extreme satisfaction every time he finished his sales pitch. Yep, Bradley the door-to-door insurance salesman was now the North Carolina Commissioner of Insurance *and* a Republican.

20

The other ladies were beside themselves when I told them the next day about my connection to the commissioner of insurance. I hadn't intended to reveal just exactly how I knew him, but well, pride got the better of me, I suppose. I've never been shy about my past, and it simply wasn't in my nature to shortchange my personal achievements. I was quite the little number in my youth, and I wanted these ladies to know it. That said, I might have pumped Bradley up to have been a bigger deal in the insurance industry at the time than he really was.

"How long has it been since you've seen him," Rebecca asked, genuinely curious.

"Probably close to forty years. I have to do the math to be sure, but I distinctly remember him wearing those long-sleeved polo shirts with the white collars on them. You know, very 1980s."

My daughter was forty years old, so technically it had been over forty years since I had laid eyes on the man. But as proud as I was of my youthful conquests, I wasn't quite ready to share with the ladies just how many I had had and that I didn't know which one of them had fathered my daughter. It could have been Bradley, for all I knew. Or Randy, or Dean, or Michael. I was pretty sure it was one of those four. The other possibilities simply didn't quite fit into the timeline. Nine months is nine months, give or take a few weeks. No, the other men in my life at the time were all outside of that window. It had to be one of the four.

"And you say he's running for governor now?" Rebecca asked.

"Yes, that's what I said. Really, Rebecca, where have you been? It was all over the news yesterday. Aren't you Ivy League professors supposed to keep up with current events? Isn't that what you're supposed to be known for? Keeping a pulse on the goings on in civic life?"

"I was a philosophy professor, not a political science professor. Metaphysics was my area of focus, where my research was centered, and about which I taught my classes."

"Meta-what?" Anna Lee asked, which I was grateful for, since I had no clue what Rebecca was talking about.

"Metaphysics," Rebecca repeated. "Metaphysics deals with concepts and theories regarding identity, knowing, causation, time, and space."

We all looked at her blankly.

"Here's an example. Take a little boy who steals a candy bar from a convenience store when he's six years old. The same boy grows up to be a man and eventually has a family of his own. When someone asks him if he ever stole something, he says no."

"Well, he's obviously lying," I said.

"Is he, though?" Rebecca prodded. "What if he truly does not remember stealing that candy bar when he was six years old. Now we have a situation where one version of this man stole a candy bar and another version of this man doesn't remember stealing that candy bar. So the question is, are these two people one and the same? Is their identity the same when one committed an act that the other does not remember?"

My head was spinning now, but I asked, "Who the hell cares whether the adult version of the boy remembers stealing a candy bar when he was actually that boy? And is this really what you were paid to ponder for forty years?"

"Here's another way of thinking about it," Rebecca continued, unfazed by my subtle accusation that she had wasted forty years of her life. "Is memory tied with identity? How often have we heard from caregivers of dementia patients that, at a certain stage, the person they're caring for is no longer the person they once knew? The person afflicted with the disease cannot remember even basic things or communicate in even the simplest of words. So again, I ask you if memory is tied with identity?"

I looked around at the others for help, but they remained silent. I was on my own.

"I'm still not completely sure I'm following what you're saying, but I think I'd have to answer that, yes, the man and the boy are one and the same. If memory is tied to identity, is it the only thing? Is memory all we have in the end? Is memory what defines us?"

"Not necessarily," Rebecca replied. "So what else?"

"Well, what about experiences? What about the impact that a person has on others throughout their lifetime? Doesn't that count for anything?" I asked.

"Go on," she continued. "Game this out for me."

"Okay, so instead of a man who steals a candy bar and doesn't remember doing so thirty years later, how about a teacher? If a teacher teaches for thirty years, but doesn't remember every single student they taught or every interaction they had during their career, then what? Can you say that this teacher didn't actually teach the students that they don't remember teaching? Would that mean that the students they don't remember teaching were taught by someone else? Because I'm not sure I could agree with that."

"You're really cooking now!" she said in encouragement.

"What I think is that the teacher's identity doesn't have to be tied solely to their own memories of who they taught. Their identity is defined as much by the impact they had on all of their students, whether they remember teaching those students or not. How could any teacher who taught for thirty years be expected to remember each and every student?"

"So what you're saying, Millie, is that you believe identity isn't about memory alone but about experiences. Experiences of their own and the experiences of those with whom their lives have interacted."

"I suppose I am."

"Now, let's discuss a more relevant example to our cause. The identity of politicians," Rebecca suggested.

I was a little uneasy about delving into the minds of politicians in such mixed company, but I was certainly intrigued.

"I think we can all agree Representative Lassiter isn't about to come out and say that she doesn't remember being a Democrat. That would be too far-fetched. But if she finds herself in unfriendly journalistic waters, and an incisive reporter asks her about her various past positions that are in conflict with her new party, she could very well say that she never really held those beliefs personally. She might even argue that her campaign website and literature, plus the speeches she may have given over the years, were all the work of her staff."

"Perhaps," Anna Lee said, "but wouldn't that call her integrity into question? What I mean is, if she says she didn't believe what she said she believed then, how would she be able to convince anyone that the beliefs she espouses now are genuinely held? I reckon that would be a terrible position for any politician to be in. To not have the trust of her voters. It would, in my opinion, require an extraordinary suspension of disbelief for her voters to simply accept what she says now as her authentic morals and principles."

"There's an old saying," Rebecca offered, "that I think might apply here. People are willing to overlook your shortcomings if they like you. Now, her former supporters would sooner spit fire at her than speak to her. But her new supporters? All of a sudden, she's given them with her singular switch the ability to see their agenda enacted with a now-powerless opposition. They like what she's done for them, so they will overlook her past positions. Hell, they probably won't even give them a second thought. She's their friend now, and they are now hers as well."

This conversation was depressing me. I long ago gave up on expecting much from our elected leaders, but I still wanted them to at least pretend to have principles. You know, for appearances, if nothing more. I'll take a false sense of security over no sense of security any day of the week. Well, no that's not true. I've always prided myself on living my life within the confines of reality. No fantasy world in which everyone is as they seem. Not for me.

"So," I said, "the question is whether Republican Alicia Lassiter is still the same person as Democratic Alicia Lassiter was. I think the answer is yes. I don't give a damn about her memory. I care about her principles. She clearly has none and never did. Therefore, she's the same person."

"I don't think that's fair," Lanie interjected. "I believe her principles have changed. It's a well-known fact that people get more conservative as they age. What's that old expression?

Something like young liberals accuse older conservatives of having no heart, and older conservatives accuse young liberals of having no brain. So, now she's got a brain! Sorry you never developed one, Rebecca. And you, too, Millie."

I knew she was joking about that last part, so I let it go. Rebecca, on the other hand, didn't. She lit into Lanie like only an Ivy League professor could, spouting off one esoteric theory after another to prove her intelligence. She had taken the bait and was going to make us all suffer as a result.

"Perhaps we should steer the conversation back toward our mission," Anna Lee suggested. "We don't have much time."

"Right you are," I added. "So, let's see. We have a venue. We have a date. We have built-in catering. We've confirmed that the party-switcher is going to attend. We really need to focus on getting a headliner now."

"What about that insurance commissioner you mentioned earlier?" Anna Lee asked. "Perhaps you might consider reaching out to him. Now that he's announced that he's running for governor, you could use that as an opening. Maybe something along the lines of wanting to reconnect with him after all these years upon seeing his image on TV. And then you could gently, and I do mean gently, mention our little fundraiser we're throwing and that you thought he'd be the perfect politician to draw a crowd."

I asked Lanie if she knew him, figuring the invitation would be better received from someone he had been in contact with more recently than forty years ago. She said she didn't, and I had to restrain myself from pointing out that she might not be quite as well connected as she's led us to believe up until this point. So, it sounded like it was, indeed, going to fall on my shoulders to reach out. I just wasn't sure how. Never having had much use for politicians in the past, I wasn't sure how to contact him. Did I need to contact his office? Or perhaps his campaign? He must have already hired a campaign chair before launching his bid for the governorship.

"Before I agree to this, I have one concern," I said. "What do I say? What I mean is, since I'm not a Republican, unless I can talk to Bradley myself, will whoever I speak with be able to tell I'm not a Republican? I don't want to blow my cover."

"All you have to do is talk like Lanie does, high-pitched and fast," Rebecca laughed.

"I don't talk like that," Lanie quipped too quickly. "And even if I did, so what?"

"Oh, never mind," I said. "I'll try speaking like my daughter does. She and her husband are both Republicans."

"My word," Anna Lee said, "that apple fell pretty far from its tree now, didn't it?"

I had never cared about politics, so I never cared that she married a Republican and then became one herself. What I did care about is that she stuck me in a retirement home faster than I could blink an eye instead of housing me until my own home was finished being rebuilt. But maybe her Republicanism might actually come in handy. I wasn't so sure Lanie would be able to fill all fifty seats at the fundraiser, so my daughter and her husband could take two of those. And I was betting some of the other partners in his firm were also Republicans. We didn't have to fill all fifty seats with influential ones, just rich ones.

"Millie," Lanie said, "if you want, I'll reach out to Commissioner Williams's campaign and see if he'd be available."

I thanked her for the offer but told her I'd take care of it one way or another. I liked Bradley back in the day, and it'd be fun to try to reconnect with him. I needed to, oh, I don't know, make sure I act my age or something. Show him that I've matured into a breathtaking, vibrant young senior citizen.

"Are you sure?" she asked, apparently unconvinced that I could get the job done on my own.

I reiterated that I'd handle the matter, and while she clearly still had her doubts, she relented and dropped the subject.

"Perhaps," Anna Lee suggested, "we might want to talk about the menu for the evening. We do want to be sure to plan a meal that will leave everyone's taste buds fully satisfied."

"Why?" Rebecca asked. "All we care about is getting the attendees there in the first place. They'll have to pay when they purchase their tickets, right? So, who cares if we serve them fillet mignon or a bunch of burgers in cardboard boxes? So long as they've paid to get in and we, I mean, Representative Lassiter's campaign has their money, right? No need for Lanie to put out more than she has to."

"Excuse me?" Lanie asked in alarm.

"Money, I mean," Rebecca clarified. "No need for you to put out more money than is absolutely necessary."

After an uncomfortably long pause, Lanie drew out of her purse a copy of the catering menu from the country club so we could discuss further. Being a member, she had a built-in advantage over the rest of us, having sampled many of the options herself over the years, and she made sure we all knew it.

"For appetizers," she said, "I suggest we order a couple of their platters. Some crudités…that's veggies and dip for those here with a less sophisticated upbringing."

She was looking directly at me. I rolled my eyes.

"A shrimp platter," she continued, "a charcuterie board…that's a meat and cheese platter, again for those here with…"

"Yes, yes, I get it," I said. "You're high society. I'm gutter trash. Move along before I drag you down into my gutter with me."

"So we should probably have an open bar, at least for the cocktail hour," she added without missing a beat. "Cash bar afterward."

Anna Lee looked at her in surprise at the mention of a cash bar. Apparently, this wasn't how the old aristocracy in Alabama did things. She thought a cash bar was tacky, but I had to side with Lanie on this one. If one of the attendees gets too drunk on free liquor and then crashes their car on the way home, you know who'd be held liable.

"A seasonal salad with crushed walnuts, crumbled bleu cheese, and a light vinaigrette, followed by a choice of mustard-glazed chicken or a rib eye steak. Mashed potatoes and asparagus on the side," Lanie added.

"What about dessert?" I asked.

"Chocolate lava cake with vanilla ice cream and a dash of caramel syrup."

"Are you sure you don't want me to bake a batch of special brownies?" I offered. "It would save on money."

Lanie ignored my suggestion and looked at the other ladies for approval of the menu. She didn't care what I thought, and that was fine with me. The others nodded their heads in agreement. So, now we had our menu.

21

Well, the next morning I had a change of heart. You know the old saying, "go big or go home." So, instead of trying to contact Bradley or his campaign by phone, I decided to track him down in person. I found out where the department of insurance building was located, took a shower, gussied myself up in my blue suit, and then had a panic attack. I don't have panic attacks. I cause other people to have panic attacks, but I don't have them myself. Except, now I did, and I didn't know why. True, I hadn't seen the man in forty years, but so what? True, I wasn't a Republican and was going to attempt to pretend to be one, but so what? No, something else was bothering me.

I was about to call the whole thing off when my phone rang. Lanie was on the other end of the call and wanted to know if I'd like to do a practice session with her so she could critique what I was planning to say. I told her she could do one better and come with me to Raleigh to see the man in person. She was surprised but pleased and said she'd pick me up in a half hour. She was already showered and simply needed to upgrade her attire for the occasion. I thanked her and ended the call. I wasn't looking forward to being stuck in a car alone with Lanie, but I realized I wasn't as "up" to the task as I had thought.

A half hour later, Lanie showed up in her Lexus, and we hit the road to Raleigh. I mean, it wasn't that great a distance, being only one city over from Springtime Pastures, so it's not like we were going on a road trip or anything. But still, twenty minutes in the car with Lanie wasn't on my fun bingo card for the day. Forty minutes, if you count the round trip.

I've never cared all that much about whether others like me or not. I've always marched to the beat of my own drummer. So, I don't know what came over me when, halfway to Raleigh, I asked Lanie what her problem was with me.

"Millie," she said, "you're just, well, special. Like, I don't quite know what to do with you or how to relate to you. You know we're not at all alike."

"I think we can agree on that," I replied. "But it's something more with me. At least that's what my psychic abilities are telling me."

"Oh, so now you're a psychic. Bravo, Millie, as if you couldn't get any stranger."

I was joking about the psychic part, but that she took what I said seriously grated on my last nerve. It's like she's incapable of letting loose and going with the flow.

"Lanie, it was a joke. Lighten up a bit. It'll do you some good. But getting back to my original question, I want specifics. What is it about me that you don't like? And please spare me the hyperbolic crap about our different social classes or stations in life. The way I see it, when we're both dead and buried in the ground, or cremated if that's your preference, no one is going to remember which one of us had more money or had the perfect children or the perfect house or the perfect breasts. Incidentally, does silicone biodegrade? Anyway, ashes to ashes and dust to dust, as they say. And no, your dust isn't going to be any sparklier than mine. A hundred years from now, whatever differences we had won't amount to a hill of beans."

"When did I ever say I didn't like you?" she asked sincerely.

"You didn't have to. You've shown it in a million different ways. Like accusing me of killing Scott or at least preventing you from saving his life. You had no proof that I was in any way involved in his death, and you refused to accept that he was beyond saving by the time you got there. It's like you don't believe a word I say. You've taken every opportunity you've ever had to put me in my place, beneath you."

"I don't hate you, Millie," she said wistfully, her voice trailing off at the end, leaving me an invitation to continue.

"Then what?" I asked.

She didn't answer immediately. We were getting closer to downtown, and I knew she needed to concentrate on where she was going. Downtown Raleigh is a maze of one-way streets, and if you don't know your way around, you're liable to get lost, or worse. I know from experience. Years ago, I came downtown to do a little research at the Government and Heritage Library. I can't for the life of me remember what I was looking for, but I'll never forget the fateful wrong turn I made down one of those one-way streets. I nearly crashed head on into an elderly couple in a big Lincoln. I ended up driving my car up onto the sidewalk to avoid them, but it was a very close call, and I was thoroughly shaken up afterward.

We continued to ride in silence while Lanie turned toward our destination and began looking for a parking spot on the street. There were a couple of parking lots she could have turned into, but she seemed intent on avoiding them. I supposed the parking lots were more costly than street parking was, so I didn't put up a fuss. She found a spot not far away from the insurance building and backed into it. I had to give her credit for being able to parallel park her car—a skill I never mastered myself.

"Millie," she said, turning toward me after shutting off the ignition. "I meant what I said. I don't hate you. I think, as much as it pains me to admit it, I'm a little envious of you."

I didn't know what to say, so I let her continue.

"You're resilient. You take whatever lemons life throws your way and squeeze them into lemonade. Nothing ever gets you down. You're like one of those inflatable dolls that rights itself every time someone lands a punch."

"I don't think anyone has ever described me in those terms before, but I'll take it as a compliment. What I don't understand is why you don't see yourself in the same light. You go out of your way to tell people how happy you are and what a fulfilling life you've led."

Now, I knew that her life was far from perfect. But she didn't know that I knew, so I figured I had better play dumb until she decided to unburden herself of this façade she'd created. I didn't have to play dumb for long, however.

"My life isn't as perfect as I've let on. People at Springtime Pastures don't think I know that my husband cheats on me every chance he gets. But I do, and I know you do, as well. I'm not upset that everyone else tried to keep me in the dark about it, either. No, the problem is I've spent most of my adult life being a devoted wife and mother. Without my family, I don't know who I am. I don't know that I could survive on my own. I'm not like you."

I wasn't prepared for such honesty from her, so it took me a minute to respond.

"Don't sell yourself short, Lanie," I finally said. "I think you're confusing ability with fear. Most people can find a way to survive on their own if they have to. Some choose to live independently like Rebecca. Others are forced to, like Anna Lee when her husband died. Look, I'm not suggesting that you divorce your husband if that's not what you want to do. But let's face facts. You're getting on in years. What do you want the rest of your life to look like? Do you want to go on pretending everything is perfect when it isn't? How many more times will you simply look the other way when your husband wanders? Oh, and just so we're clear, I would never sleep with your husband. You may not think much of me, but that's one line I've never crossed and would never cross. And I think I can say the same for Rebecca and Anna Lee."

"Fortunately, none of you are my husband's type," she said a little flippantly, but I didn't let her tone bother me.

"No, I suppose not. We're all too smart for him," I laughed, trying to lighten the mood a little.

"Are you suggesting that I'm not? Because let me tell you, Millie Holt, that I could have been something. Got a 1420 on the SAT. Even went to college for a year before dropping out to support my own mother after my father passed away and left her destitute."

"Is that why you married a doctor? To provide for you and your mother?"

"Well, he wasn't a doctor yet. He was in medical school, which I helped pay for. It was what you might consider a long-term investment. And it paid off."

"In money and financial security, perhaps, but what about your happiness? When was the last time you remember truly being happy?"

She took a moment to ponder my question and then answered, "Probably the day my last child was born. There was something magical, even spiritual about bringing a new life into this world for me."

I could relate to that. Giving birth to my own daughter was one of the happiest days of my life, even though I had no idea how I was going to support the two of us at the time. It didn't matter. I had this beautiful little creature in my arms who I knew I was going to love until my dying day. Of course, I didn't know then that she would one day kick me out of her house simply because I didn't fit neatly into the lifestyle that she and her husband had tried to create for their own family. But that was beside the point now.

"Listen," I said, surprising myself with what I was about to suggest, "I'm not the type of person who tells other people if they should or shouldn't stay in their marriages. But if you ever decide that you need a place to escape to, to figure things out, you can stay with me once my house is done being rebuilt."

She started laughing.

"No, I'm serious. I'm actually offering my place as a refuge for you, should you ever need it."

"Now why would I want to come stay with you?" she asked somewhat seriously.

"Even if you never take me up on it, does it help to know that you have a backup plan? A place where you can go, no questions asked?"

She said she thought the heat was getting to me and that she shouldn't have turned the car off before we were ready to make our way into the building. And then, after an uncomfortably long pause, she took my hand in hers, squeezed it, and thanked me.

We walked into the department of insurance building, a concrete structure stretching ten stories or so into the sky, that probably dated to the 1960s, and asked for directions to the commissioner's office. The security guard asked us if we had an appointment with Commissioner Williams, and thanks to my quick thinking, I said that we did, indeed, and that he was expecting us. The guard was skeptical and asked us for our photo IDs so he could call upstairs to inquire about our alleged appointment. All we could do was pray that Bradley would recognize my name.

Unfortunately, it was Bradley's administrative assistant who fielded the call from the security guard, and since she had no idea who I was, she must have told the security guard not to let us upstairs. The next thing we knew, he was trying to escort us out of the building, but as luck would have it, Bradley himself walked in the door, and as our eyes met, immediate recognition washed over his face. Well, sort of. Based on his expression, he couldn't quite place me, but he must have known that our paths had crossed at some point in his past.

"It's Millie," I said as I realized he wasn't going to be able to place a name with my face without a little help. "Millie Holt. It's certainly been a while. But time has been good to you!"

It took him several more seconds to place my name and my face within the context of his own past, but he eventually got there. Surprise spread across his face, and then a wistful glance into my eyes told me all I needed to know. He was going to be putty in my hands, and this time, I was going to be in the driver's seat. No finishing his sales pitch before I was ready, especially since I was going to be the one pitching him!

"I can't believe you're here," he said. "How long has it been now?"

"Oh, long enough," I said, not wanting to linger on our respective ages now.

I started to introduce him to Lanie, but when I glanced over at her, she was practically frozen. I nudged her a little, and she came to life, introducing herself and explaining that she was a big fan of his work in trying to institute work requirements for Medicaid recipients. It was all I could do to not roll my eyes. She and I were never going to agree on health care as a universal right, and I didn't want to hurt our chances of getting Bradley to agree to headline our fundraiser. Plus, I couldn't afford to blow my cover. So, I put politics aside, for a moment, and pretended to nod in agreement.

Bradley took us both up to his office, his administrative assistant giving us the stink eye as we breezed past her, and we sat down in a couple of very comfortable chairs on one side of his expansive mahogany desk. His office was on the top floor and had a breathtaking view of the downtown skyline.

"So, what can I do for you ladies?" he asked.

"Well, it's like this," I said, not wanting to waste any time. "We're putting together a fundraiser for Representative Alicia Lassiter, now that she's switched parties and will need some help getting reelected in her blue district. We were wondering if you'd be willing to come speak at the event. We know it's short notice, but given your recent announcement regarding your campaign for governor, we thought you might like the opportunity to speak in front of some of the wealthiest and most well-connected members of your party. I mean, our party, of course."

He raised an eyebrow at my near slip. Damn. I really should have let Lanie do all the talking. That's why I brought her along in the first place.

"You're a Republican, Millie?" he asked, flabbergasted. "I never would have guessed. You always struck me as more of the Green party, hippie type."

"Oh, no. Well, maybe in my distant past. But now I'm as red as they get. I've seen the light," I said, trying to sound like I believed what I was saying.

"Go figure," he responded, not totally convinced.

"It's true," Lanie said, coming to my defense. "She's seen the errors of her ways, and I can personally vouch for her. She's as much a Republican as you and I are. She firmly believes in small government, lower taxes, and living the American dream. She's even a successful entrepreneur, selling various herbal supplements to an ever increasingly devoted clientele. They rave about her products!"

Of course, Bradley knew exactly what Lanie was referring to, having partaken with me on multiple occasions back in the day. Perhaps I should have filled her in on more of the details of our past connection. But I didn't and had to make the best of a slightly awkward situation now.

"Yes, well, anyway," I interrupted. "What do you say, Bradley? Are you in?"

He asked us when the fundraiser was scheduled to take place, and after we confirmed the date with him, he said he'd he happy to attend but had one condition. I had to agree to go on a date with him beforehand.

This was why I had the panic attack earlier, I realized. I was afraid he'd want another go on the Millie Holt merry-go-round, and I wasn't interested. When I hesitated, Lanie offered to go on the date with him instead! I couldn't believe it and had to discreetly remind her that she was a married woman by subtly rubbing my ring finger. She got the hint and backed off.

"Listen, Bradley, I would love to go on a date with you. Really, I would. But I have such a busy schedule between now and the fundraiser. I'm not sure I'd be able to squeeze you in."

"Oh, the Millie I remember never had trouble squeezing me in, if you know what I mean," he laughed.

Lanie didn't get the joke, and I was not about to explain it to her. I told Bradley I'd do the best that I could, but that I wasn't in a position to commit to the date right now. He then suggested something shorter and more casual than a date, and I told him I'd see what I could do and that I'd be back in touch with him. I knew what he was after, and while I was pleased to know I still had "it" in his eyes, I wasn't about to enter into a pay for play situation. I would agree to this little rendezvous now and then back out at the last minute, but only after we started publicizing the fundraiser so he couldn't cancel on us if I didn't hold up my end of the bargain.

22

Lanie and I were pretty pleased with ourselves when we met with the other ladies for lunch the next day. I had requested that we do lunch here in the B-Block dining room so that Chessy could join us. Since she was going to serve as the entertainment for the fundraiser, I figured the others would want to meet her beforehand. So, there we were, the five of us sitting around a table meant for four, planning our little hearts out.

We took stock of our current situation and realized we had checked off most of the items on our to-do list. All we really had to do was send out the invites, which Anna Lee had procured on a rush order from a calligrapher she knew back in Alabama. Okay, they weren't hand-written calligraphy, but they were printed to look as if they were. Very classy, done in a red, white, and blue motif. Well, the paper was white anyway.

Lanie brought her address book and started labeling envelopes as we talked. She wasn't kidding. She really had connections. We figured that, with fifty seats, we'd probably need to invite at least sixty-five, especially on such short notice. The event was only a couple of weeks away at this point, and undoubtedly, some of the people on Lanie's list would already have other commitments made. I hadn't yet reached out to my daughter, but that was on the agenda for this afternoon. Not that I was particularly looking forward to speaking with her.

Chessy surprised us, though, with some information on the coroner's report regarding Scott's death. I was under the impression that an autopsy wasn't going to be performed, but given the mysterious nature of Scott's passing, his family relented and allowed it to proceed. Rebecca asked her how she had managed to come by this information, but Chessy declined to provide specifics. They all knew she was a forensic psychologist in a previous life, as she made sure to tell them as much when she was introducing herself. But for whatever reason, Chessy decided to keep her cards close to her chest. All I could do was guess that she still had connections to various people in positions of power within the law enforcement community.

Anyway, Chessy explained that the coroner's report revealed that Scott had died of a myocardial infarction. I had to ask what that meant, and she explained that a heart attack brought about his sudden death. All I could think was that at least we had an answer now. But Chessy continued her explanation, informing us that based on the autopsy, he was likely dead before he hit the water.

I asked her how the coroner could have determined that he'd had the heart attack on the pool deck or possibly somewhere else and not *in* the water. Like, maybe he had a charley horse or something and was too far away from the side of the pool. She said it likely had something to do with the tissue examination of his lungs. Well, this didn't clear things up one bit, so she continued. Apparently, there are certain physiological functions that occur if one is struggling in any sort of body of water, and eventually, if one can't reach the surface to breathe, the lungs can override the brain and attempt to breathe without permission, thus sucking in a whole bunch of water.

Still having trouble wrapping my mind around the concept, she explained that, when the lungs actively breathe in water, there's an effect that, if the body expires in the process, remains. But since no such effect was found in Scott's lungs, he must have died before hitting the water. I asked Chessy for the precise medical terminology, more for my own edification than anything else, but she couldn't remember.

What Chessy had presented, though, seemed to pretty conclusively indicate that Scott was on land when he died and then somehow ended up in the water, face down. Whether he was steps away from the pool when he died, or whether he died somewhere else and was then transported to the pool, we didn't know. Either was possible. He was scheduled to be at the pool that morning for our water aerobics class, so it's not like he was found somewhere he shouldn't have been. But at the same time, if this wasn't an accidental death, someone could have killed him elsewhere and then dumped his body in the pool. They'd likely have known that he was supposed to be there that morning, which would certainly lower any suspicions that foul play was involved.

I asked Chessy if she thought it possible for Scott to have been facing outward from the pool before falling in back-first, given that I eventually found him face down and not face up. She said anything was possible, but that her past experience in murder cases made that unlikely. So, Scott was likely facing the pool when he had the heart attack, passed away, and then fell in. Assuming of course, that he had died mere steps from the water's edge. I still thought he was too young to have had a spontaneous heart attack, but maybe he had one of those widow-maker hearts and didn't know it. Seemed like a bit of a stretch, though, given his former Olympic career. Surely someone would have caught any sort of related condition somewhere along the way.

I reminded everyone present that Julie hadn't indicated that Scott had had any pre-existing health conditions, and I was promptly reminded by the four of them together that he simply might not have told her if he knew. Fair point. But to get involved with someone and not inform them that you have a condition that could potentially take your life at any moment seemed like a pretty shady thing to do. But maybe he wasn't as serious about Julie as she was about him. No, wait. Strike that. He *definitely* wasn't as serious about her. I thought about those emails we found from his former girlfriends. He had a pattern, and Julie may have simply been the latest victim to fall prey to his charms.

What I still couldn't wrap my mind around, however, was what could have caused his heart attack if we assume that it wasn't due to natural causes. I took a poll of the other ladies to see whether there was any consensus regarding the physical location of Scott's death. The deck of the pool or somewhere else. We were all pretty much on the same page about that, thankfully. It just seemed too far-fetched for someone to have caused him to have a heart attack and then transported his body to the pool for someone else to find. Not that I've ever been involved in the death of another human being, but if I were, I would have found some other way to dispose of the body. Some way that would have made it less likely to be discovered. Like the meat grinder in *Sweeney Todd*, perhaps.

We all also seemed to come to the consensus that Scott hadn't suffered a random heart attack. Something must have set it off. Or someone. And whatever happened likely wasn't medically induced, since those pills Chessy had had tested for us turned out to be exactly what they were supposed to be.

I knew we were operating without much evidence to go on, but I took some comfort in the knowledge that we were all united on this. Even Lanie had to agree that someone other than myself was most likely involved. I kept coming back to Mr. Lassiter as the likeliest of suspects. Probably because he was the only suspect we currently had in our crosshairs.

Once we exhausted the topic of Scott's death-by-heart-attack, we moved on to the next most important subject at hand. Chessy wanted us to help nail down her set list for the fundraiser. Which songs would she sing? Which of Sondheim's tunes would garner the best response from our particular audience? Rebecca suggested "Rich and Happy" from *Merrily We Roll Along*. Chessy reminded everyone that "Rich and Happy" was meant to be sung as a duet, and she wasn't sure she could pull it off. I told her she did a wonderful job with "A Little Priest" a few days ago, also a duet.

Lanie suggested adding "A Weekend in the Country" from *A Little Night Music*, figuring it'd play well with the upwardly mobile crowd we were expecting. Chessy shot that idea down pretty quickly, though, given that the piece was meant for an entire ensemble. I suggested, as a joke, that she sing "Send in the Clowns" instead. Not because of the lyrics, but because of the title! Everyone laughed, but the more we thought about it, the more we warmed to the idea. It's one of the most beautiful, heart-rending ballads ever sung on the stage.

As a grand finale, I suggested "The Ladies Who Lunch" from *Company*. Everyone approved. No one could find fault with the lyrics. It has a little of something for everyone. The housewives, the career girls, the lushes, the well-educated. It was perfect! Plus, it takes real talent to pull it off, especially if the singer has to sing a cappella. And since we weren't yet sure whether we'd be able to pipe in any musical accompaniment, I was a little unsure whether Chessy would agree to do it. But she did and then did us one better. She said she knew an accompanist whom she thought she could cajole into attending.

Lanie said the country club had a grand piano, but she wasn't certain whether it could be moved into the dining room she had reserved for the event. Anna Lee suggested that she herself join the country club in short order, paying the highest membership dues possible, and making the whole thing contingent on getting that piano into the dining room for the event. Lanie said she appreciated the gesture but would try to work her own connections first. She seemed to think that she had a lot of strings to pull there, so we left her to it.

We chatted for a little while longer, and then I made my excuses and left to return to my cell. I wasn't particularly looking forward to calling my daughter, but I knew I needed to get it over with. We hadn't spoken much at all in the last month or so. She was busy with her children, and I respected that. But I felt a little abandoned here. Well, more than a little. Sure, I had made some friends apparently, finally, but I still couldn't get over the fact that my own daughter put me in a home.

After taking a couple of swigs of my contraband booze, I took my cell phone out and dialed her number. Once upon a time, she was listed in my contacts, but after she threw me in here, I decided that her name didn't deserve a place in my phone. Okay, I'm exaggerating. Her number was still stored, but I took her name out. Maybe a little petty of me, but when you get to be my age, you've earned the right to be petty now and then.

"Hello?" she said after picking up the call.

"It's your mother. You know, the one you threw in a home six months ago against her will?"

As long as I draw breath in my body, I will never let her live it down.

"Oh, hi, Mom," she said after a brief pause, probably trying to decide whether to continue the call or to cut me off at the knees.

"How are you doing on this fine day?" I asked, figuring I'd better fix my tone of voice before the whole conversation blew up and, with it, my chance to ensure we hit our max capacity for the fundraiser.

"Fine, but busy. I have to pick the kids up at school in a little while and take them to their respective after-school activities."

The older grandchild was taking tennis lessons, and the younger was enrolled in a ballet program at a dance studio nearby. I swear, these kids were the most overscheduled little beings on the face of God's green earth.

"Have I mentioned lately what a wonderful mother you are to the two of them? You've done everything right. It warms my heart to see how well you take care of their every need and desire. I hope when they grow up they appreciate all you and your husband have done for them. They are truly lucky to have such kind, caring, giving, and devoted parents."

I knew I was laying it on pretty thick. I just had to hope I was coming across sincerely.

"Who are you? And what have you done with my cranky old mother?" she asked.

"Oh, silly billy," I said, laughing. "I was joking earlier. No, I've found true happiness here at Springtime Pastures, and I owe that happiness all to your wise and sound judgment that this was a better place for me to reside in while my house is being rebuilt than your own home. I have my own space here, and I've made some wonderful, lifelong friends whom I hope to stay in touch with even after I leave. Although, to tell you the truth, I've been thinking about seeing whether I might stay on here a while longer."

"Really?" she asked. "Not that I want to burst your bubble, but have you thought about how you might pay your own way to stay? As much as my husband and I would love to keep footing the bill for your residency at Springtime Pastures, it isn't something we had planned on doing long-term."

Well, of course I hadn't thought about the financial implications of staying. I wasn't planning on staying period. But now I had to think of a quick response.

"I have it all planned out," I lied, trying to buy a little more time. "You see, it's like this."

"Like what?" she asked after I paused, hoping that some sort of divine inspiration would strike.

"I was thinking that, once my house is done being built, I could rent it out. Property values have gone way up, and I bet I could get double my mortgage payment in rent. I'd rent the house out and use the extra income to pay my way here."

"Mom, do you have any idea how much we're paying for you to live there?"

"Well, no, but given the, um, cramped quarters and the middling-at-best food, it can't be that much. Plus, I do still have my social security check to help, and I might think about starting a business of my own. A legal business. Like caregiving for some of the other residents beyond what the facility provides. You know, like a private nurse, to make some extra dough. Or maybe I could work as a driver for some of the more infirm residents either here in B-Block or elsewhere in the community."

I knew I was spinning a pretty tall tale here, but what else could I do?

"Well, it's your life, Mom, but whatever you do, please understand that we're not in a position to help financially indefinitely."

"I hear you loud and clear. But anyway, that's not what I was calling you about. I was calling to invite you and your husband to a little fundraiser that some of the ladies here and I are planning."

"Oh? What's the cause?"

"It's for that lovely lady in the legislature who recently became a Republican. Alicia Lassiter. I think she's terrific, and I want to do what I can to help her get reelected next year."

"Wait, let me get this straight. You, a woman who's never had a political bone in her body, are now actively fundraising for a politician? What are you going to tell me next, Mom? That pink elephants have suddenly sprouted wings and are flying about in the sky?"

"Oh, the ladies I've become friends with have shown me the error of my ways," I said, and then with a stroke of genius, I continued, "we need more Republicans in the legislature so they can lower our taxes. I'm going to need my taxes lowered a bit so I can stay here at Springtime Pastures."

"I have to say I'm pleasantly surprised, Mom. When and where is this fundraiser, and how much are you expecting us to chip in? What's the plan?"

So, I gave her all the details, and to my surprise, she didn't blanche at the mention of the five thousand dollars a plate price tag. I asked her if she thought any of her husband's partners might also be interested in attending, and she said she'd have him ask around. She even offered to take me shopping for a suitable outfit, which I graciously accepted. A fancy suit or dress definitely wasn't in my budget!

23

The next few weeks went by in a blur. We were all busy getting ready for the fundraiser. Decisions had to be made on the final menu, decorations, flower centerpieces for the tables, and a host of other minor little details too trivial to even bother mentioning. Lanie had been successful in arranging for the country club's grand piano to be moved into the dining room, and Chessy was able to confirm the booking of her accompanist. We also had every seat in the joint spoken for, a mix of Lanie's political connections and my son-in-law's legal connections. Everything was going our way.

I finally had to let Julie in on our plans, though I omitted the part about Mr. Lassiter being overly smitten with Scott. When I explained what we were going to do, she was on board. She said that anything we could do to figure out what happened to her poor, beloved Scotty was "A-OK" in her book. She didn't even object to allowing Chessy to leave the premises.

Oh, and the biggest news of all was that, two days ago, the contractor overseeing the rebuilding of my house phoned me to let me know it had passed all the necessary inspections and was safe for me to inhabit once more. I couldn't wait. As much as I had grown fond of my coconspirators, even Lanie, I was ready for my jailbreak moment. Prison food isn't for the feeble or faint of heart.

One thing I hadn't planned on, though, was the purchasing of new furniture. I called my daughter and son-in-law for help with that, of course, but they asked me what I had done with all the insurance money I got after the fire. Well, I didn't know what they were talking about. Aside from paying for the reconstruction and a small monthly allowance for temporary housing, I hadn't gotten anything. My son-in-law asked me if he could take a look at my policy, saying that I should have gotten a lump sum of some sort to replace my personal belongings, including furniture. But, as I'm sure you can guess, the policy went up in flames with the rest of my house. He said he'd call the insurance company for me and make some inquiries.

Anyway, the evening of the fundraiser had finally arrived. I had spent the afternoon at Anna Lee's getting all dolled up. As promised, she had hired a stylist and makeup artist to give Rebecca and me a whole new look so that Mr. Lassiter wouldn't immediately recognize us from that fiasco at the library. This whole new look for me included a bucketload of makeup and a temporary rinse to my hair, turning it from its natural silver to a beautiful reddish-blond color. I hated going through all this fuss, especially for a single evening, but I looked damn good when the professionals were done with me. Rebecca too.

After returning to my cell, I ate a quick snack and took a few swigs of my contraband booze for nerves before getting into the dress and shoes my daughter helped me pick out. I didn't look like myself at all, but as they say, when you're going into a room full of rich Republicans, you might as well look the part. And look the part I did indeed. Right down to the jewelry Anna Lee lent me from her personal collection, after making me sign a blood oath to return it all upon the conclusion of the night's festivities.

I was just about to head out the door to meet Chessy and Julie at the designated rendezvous point when my cell phone rang. Fishing it out of the sparkly purse Lanie had lent me for the occasion, I looked at the caller ID and answered the call.

"Lanie," I said, "is everything all right? I'm heading out now."

"My car won't start, and my husband is missing in action. He was supposed to come with me, but he and his car are nowhere to be found. I'm afraid I won't be able to make it tonight."

Was she kidding me? Had she never heard of a taxi before? Or one of those newer ride app services? Or asking one of us to pick her up? Anna Lee had offered to rent a limousine so we could all ride to the fundraiser in style, but Lanie had adamantly refused to participate. I actually began to suspect that maybe she had planned all along not to attend.

"All right, what the hell is going on?" I asked. "Because I don't believe for a moment that your car won't start. You keep that car in pristine condition. And even if you're telling me the truth, there are plenty of other modes of transportation you could use."

"I...I don't think I can do this," she said, not bothering to put up a fight. "We're using the attendees, pumping them for more information on Mr. Lassiter. Many of them are my personal friends."

"No, they're not," I snapped. "They pretend to be your friends because they want your campaign contribution dollars. They're all the same. Democrat, Republican, whatever. All they want from you is your money, and they are willing to do just about anything to get it."

"Now, that's not fair. I've known some of them for years, even decades. Invited them to my children's baptisms, birthday parties, high school graduations even."

"So, you feel like you're betraying them?"

"Exactly. I can't do this. It's like, well, if someone were to ask you to work with an undercover cop to bust an illegal weed operation. Those are your people. You'd be turning against them. These are my people."

"And how long have you been planning on ditching us at the last possible moment?"

No way was I going to let her off the hook now.

"I don't know what you mean," she responded.

"Oh, yes, you do. You'll have to forgive me, but I hardly believe that you're simply having some sort of last-minute moral crisis over what we're about to do. So, how long have you been sitting with these doubts, and how long have you been planning to back out of the actual event?"

"Since we sent out the invitations," Lanie admitted. "I was caught up in the thrill of it all when I was addressing the envelopes at lunch that day, but when I actually put them in the mailbox and sent them on their way, well, I felt this enormous sense of guilt."

"But you kept working with us on all the details. Even if you don't go tonight, you've been involved at every step of the way. And if our true motive for holding this shindig should ever be discovered, most of the attendees are going to remember your connection to the event anyway. Your name was the only one listed on the invitation as the host. Remember? So, what difference does it make if you show up tonight or not?"

"It makes a difference to me."

"How? By not looking them in the eye? Is that it? If you don't have to face them, it's like you're not using them or something?"

"Maybe. I just can't do it. I truly am sorry, and I hope the event goes well for the rest of you and that you find what you're looking for."

"Look, I don't have time to argue with you. I've gotta meet Chessy and Julie," I said as I ended the call.

After texting Rebecca a quick message apprising her of the situation, I left my room and headed toward the elevator to take me down to the first floor. We had arranged to meet at one of the back entrances so Chessy would avoid running into any of the other staff members who might question her departure from the building. She was waiting for me as planned, and we exited B-block to find Julie in her SUV mere steps away.

"We need to make a pit stop," I informed Julie as Chessy and I climbed in. "Lanie's having car trouble, so we're going to pick her up."

I figured there was no point in letting them know just yet about Lanie getting cold feet. It was more important that we get to her house before she got her wits about her enough to escape. The way I saw it, she had to have known that I'd come chasing after her. Rebecca had texted me back and was going to meet us there as well, and she said she'd call Anna Lee and update her on the current situation.

When we got to Lanie's, we found her in her Lexus, pulling out of the driveway. If only we had been there a couple of seconds sooner, we could have blocked her in, but she had managed to pull onto the street and was heading out. At this point, I had to let Chessy and Julie know what was going on and instructed Julie to follow Lanie's car. I then called Rebecca and gave her our precise location and directions on where to go to head Lanie off. She said she'd get Anna Lee back on the phone as well so we could all coordinate. I told her not to bother. I was going to initiate a three-way call so we could all coordinate more effectively.

Lanie figured out pretty quickly that we were following her and made a couple of very quick turns, hopping the curb on one of them, but she couldn't shake us. Julie was an excellent driver in this big SUV of hers, and she kept pace with Lanie through every move she made. It took a minute or two to figure out where Lanie was ultimately heading, but once I realized she was driving toward the main entrance to Springtime Pastures, I alerted Rebecca and Anna Lee. Rebecca was too far away to intercede, but Anna Lee and her big black Benz weren't. She instructed her driver to "step on it'" and then let us know she'd have him park perpendicular in the road so as to block Lanie's egress. I wasn't so sure that'd stop her, but it was the best we could do.

Sure enough, a moment later, Julie slammed on her brakes to avoid rear ending Lanie, who had stopped very suddenly, mere inches away from T-boning Anna Lee in her Benz. I instructed Julie to pull as close to Lanie as possible so she wouldn't have room enough to back up and turn around. Lanie got out of her car and marched over to the opened rear window of the Benz to have it out with Anna Lee, or perhaps the other way around. Meanwhile, the three of us got out of Julie's car, and Rebecca, having pulled up, got out of hers as well.

"Move this car!" Lanie screamed at Anna Lee, "Or I'll move it for you!"

"Dear," Anna Lee responded, "I wonder if you're having some sort of delusion in which you are under the impression that I will comply with your orders. Now, listen to me carefully. You are going to come ride with me, and we're going to have a long chat on our way to the fundraiser. Millie will drive your car there, so you won't have to worry about leaving it on the side of the road. But I am not moving my car to get out of your way, and Julie isn't going to move hers either. So the way I see it, you might as well cooperate with us. I got the gist of your concerns from Millie, but I think perhaps I can allay your worries more effectively on the ride to the country club. You know, from one queen bee to another."

I had to give Anna Lee some credit for quick thinking. She knew exactly how to get Lanie to cooperate. And it's not that I didn't understand what Lanie was going through, what she was wrestling with. Whether or not I agreed, she felt that she was about to betray people she cared for, her friends. I could only hope that Anna Lee would be able to find a way to help Lanie feel better about our mission this evening.

All we really wanted was to get more information on Mr. Lassiter. It's not like we were intentionally spying on an internal organization meeting with the intent of leaking whatever information we manage to obtain to another political party. We just wanted to know the nature of Mr. Lassiter's relationship with Scott and whether he was capable of murder, even if accidental. Was that really so much to ask for?

Anyway, Lanie did as she was told and got into the back seat of Anna Lee's Benz. Rebecca and Julie got back into their cars, and Chessy and I slipped into Lanie's. Julie had protested at first, wanting to keep a close eye on Chessy herself, but I assured her that I was more than capable of ferrying the two of us to the country club without incident.

"Millie," Chessy said as we turned out of Springtime Pastures onto the main road, "did you happen to notice that Lanie was very nicely dressed. Too nicely dressed for a woman who wasn't planning on going to a ritzy affair."

"Yes, I noticed that, as well. Between you and me, I don't think Lanie actually planned not to attend. I think this was her way of ensuring we all understood what a sacrifice she was making for our cause. She wanted us to recognize what she was potentially giving up if tonight's event goes south."

"I don't know her as well as you do, but I think she's a much more complex person than she seems on the surface. Not like me. What you see is what you get," Chessy observed.

Well, what I saw in Chessy at the moment was an eighty-year-old woman decked out in bright red sequins from head to toe. Even her shoes were sequined. But she was wise, and I began thinking about my earlier offer to Lanie to let her come stay with me if she ever decided to leave her cheating husband. Could Lanie and I become true friends over time? I mean, we had virtually nothing in common, but there was something about her that I began to admire. It takes a lot of effort to keep up appearances the way she's done. When she commits to something, she really commits to it. She's dependable, present circumstances excluded, and I needed more dependable people in my life.

"Lanie's got more layers to her than an onion," I laughed. "I'm not sure I'll live long enough to peel them all away, but it might be worth trying. I think I've misjudged her. I supposed I always thought of her as some sort of caricature. The devoted doctor's wife who was hell bent on keeping her picture-perfect life together, no matter how rotten its foundation was. But her crazy runs deeper than that. Eh, maybe crazy isn't the right word for it. She's afraid. She's afraid of what her life would look like if she lets go."

"I can relate to that. But I didn't have a choice. My husband got sick and died. I had to change, and look at me now! I live in a comfortable apartment, have three meals a day that I don't have to fix myself, and I get to do whatever I want because I have dementia, or rather because everyone *thinks* I have dementia."

"Speaking of which, I've been meaning to mention again to you that you ought to tone down your act a bit."

"And why would I do a thing like that?"

"Because they're gonna throw you into a memory care unit if you don't. You said so yourself. Just promise me this. No more stripteases in the lobby, okay?"

"Oh, well, fine. I guess you have a point there."

"And maybe tone down the outfits a bit."

"Never!"

24

I found some cash in the center console as we pulled into the country club, so I figured Lanie might as well treat us to some good old-fashioned valet parking. When we pulled up behind Anna Lee's Benz near the front door, a very nice young man with a partially shaved head and a tattoo on his face came running toward us and, once he was within reach, opened Chessy's door. After I got out myself, he met me halfway between and gave me the requisite valet ticket. I gave him a very nice tip. He was thrilled. I was thrilled. Both of us were thrilled, probably for different reasons. Body art is a particular turn-on of mine. The more tattoos the better!

But anyway, we walked into the club and were greeted by a staff member who showed us to the dining room where the fundraiser was set to take place. It had just occurred to me that I hadn't seen this particular room before. I probably should have gone with Lanie earlier to check it out for myself and was surprised I hadn't thought to do so, but I needn't have worried. The room was beautifully done with a deeply patterned taupe carpet, a sophisticated wallpaper with a mere hint of a floral motif, heavily draped windows on one wall and exquisite chandeliers hanging from above.

The tables were set with very expensive looking cream-colored coverings, and each place setting had more utensils than I knew what to do with. There was a bar set up against the far wall between two of the windows, and a stage big enough to hold its podium and the grand piano sat against the left wall. There was room in front for a small dance floor, but since no dancing was on the agenda for the evening, the space remained vacant. Probably wise as our guests were going to need an open area for mingling during the cocktail hour.

We still had a few minutes before the guests were expected to arrive, so Chessy and I made our way over to where the others were already sitting. Lanie seemed to be a little calmer than she was when I last saw her begrudgingly climbing into Anna Lee's Benz. Whatever Anna Lee said to her, I was grateful for it. We needed Lanie to help us mingle with the guests. None of the rest of us had any connections with them, save for Bradley Williams, of course. Oh, and my daughter and her husband, as well.

After going over the agenda once more and making sure we were all on the same page, I went to the bar and asked the bartender for a gin and tonic, heavy on the gin. And then I told him he might as well give me two of them. I was in a double-fisting mood tonight, and come hell or high water, I was going to succeed in my quest to get some answers about Mr. Lassiter and his murderous proclivities. Every bone in my body was telling me that he had something to do with Scott's death, and I was going to prove it.

Out of the corner of my eye, as I was heading back to the table, I noticed the first guest walking through the door into the dining room. I wouldn't have thought much of it, but something about the slightly awkward smile on his face caught my attention. I put my two drinks down on the table in front of a gaping Lanie and turned back toward the man. There was something very familiar about him. I turned back to Lanie and asked her if she knew who he was. Well, she looked at me like I had vines growing out of my ears or something, like how dare I *not* know who he was.

"That's Michael Shreves. He's the speaker of the North Carolina House of Representatives. You know, the one I wanted to headline tonight's event until you discovered you had a connection with Commissioner Williams."

I couldn't believe it. Michael Shreves, here in the flesh. The consumer products tester who was always trying to get me to rate his products. And by products, if you didn't understand me before, I mean the services he provided to me. In bed. At the end of every sexual encounter we had, he'd ask me how he did, like on a scale of one to ten. I mean, he really was a consumer products tester, but when he was with me, I was the one testing his lovemaking abilities. I tried giving him honest scores in the beginning, usually a four or a five, but his ego was just so fragile. Toward the end of our run, I was giving him straight tens to keep him from falling apart.

And now look at him. Speaker of the House! I never would have guessed that this is how he'd turn out. A politician, no less, and apparently a very successful one. Hell, I could have been Mrs. Speaker of the House if the sex were better. But I wasn't very good at dealing with mediocrity on a long-term basis, and I knew a committed relationship with him back then was out of the question. I didn't see any wife coming in with him, though, and I didn't see a wedding ring either. I supposed he hadn't had any luck finding a woman who'd put up with bad sex for fifty or sixty years. I certainly wouldn't have. But he was still pretty cute. Maybe I'd find a chance to steal him away from the night's festivities and see if he's learned a thing or two over the past four decades.

"Please don't tell me you know him," Lanie said as she tugged on my sleeve.

"Why? Are you afraid you'll find out I have more connections to influential Republicans than you do?"

She didn't respond.

"Yes, Lanie," I said. "I know Michael Shreves, or rather, I knew him once upon a time. Been decades since I've laid eyes on him, but I'd recognize that crooked smile anywhere. Even in the pale glow of the moon above a grassy pasture with nothing but a blanket between our naked bodies and the earth beneath."

Okay, I made that last part up to get a rise out of her. Michael and I never had sex in the out-of-doors. At least I don't think we did. I'll have to ask him, and since he was heading our way, I'd have the perfect opportunity.

"Speaker Shreves," Lanie said as he approached us. "So good of you to come tonight."

He nodded as she introduced the rest of our group to him, and then his eyes met mine, and it was instant recognition. He didn't know what to say, so I pretended for his sake that we were meeting for the first time. I didn't know if he was embarrassed at running into a former paramour in this particular setting or if he was simply speechless at my still breathtaking beauty. I chose to assume the latter. Fortunately, a wave of attendees started rolling in, and one of them called his name, so he left our company to go chat up the newly arrived guests, with Lanie in tow.

Chessy's accompanist arrived a few moments later, and she went off with him to discuss a set list for some background music he would play during the cocktail hour. I was grateful for her quick thinking since it hadn't occurred to me or to anyone else to provide for such music in the first place. Meanwhile, Rebecca went to the club's event manager, who was standing near the entryway, to let her know we were ready for the appetizers to be served. They were already laid out on a buffet table, but the cellophane wrappings needed to be removed.

"Come sit by me for a moment," Anna Lee said. "I haven't had a chance to express my sincere gratitude for all the work you have put into this event. Scott was a very special boy to me, and if we are able to learn anything tonight that might lead us to understand what happened to him, why he had that heart attack, I will be in your debt."

"Why, thank you," I said as I took a seat next to her. "Not bad for a girl born on the wrong side of the tracks, eh?"

"Not bad at all," she said with a wink as she took my hand in hers and squeezed it. "I am not so high and mighty that I can't admit when I'm wrong about someone. I was wrong about you. You have more class in your little pinky finger than the woman for whom we're holding this fundraiser has in her whole entire body. You have convictions, and you stick to them. Your word is as good as gold, and that goes a long, long way in my book."

"Right back at you. You're good people," I laughed, though a part of me really meant it.

Meeting Anna Lee for the first time several months ago, I was reminded of too many of the debutantes I'd had to contend with. Vapid. All about appearances. But I had misjudged her just as she had misjudged me, and I realized that now. She was far more complex than she let on.

"I heard that your house is done being rebuilt and that you'll be leaving us soon. I do hope you'll keep in touch. You'll find that when I make a friend I truly cherish, it's exceedingly difficult to—oh, what's the term the kids are using these days?—to ghost me. So don't think you're going to be off the hook from attending any more of my lunches or tea socials. And if you decide to restart your herbal supplement business, there are a number of women in my social circle who suffer from arthritis, glaucoma, and several other conditions and would benefit greatly from your services. You'd be able to make a pretty penny serving our community."

"I can't believe you know what 'ghosting' is," I laughed. "Anna Lee Benton, you are a woman full of surprises."

"I am, indeed. Even us old birds can still learn new flight patterns."

I nodded in agreement, but before I could say anything else, a finger began tapping on my right shoulder. I turned around to see who the finger belonged to.

"Hi, Mom," my daughter said.

"Darling," I said as I stood up to hug her. "So good of you to come. Where's your husband?"

"He's a bit under the weather, I'm afraid. Probably nothing more than an allergy attack, but he didn't want to expose anyone else in case it's something more serious."

"How thoughtful and considerate of him. But I am glad to see you, at least."

"I wouldn't miss this," she said. "You're up to something. I just don't know what. I'm here to keep an eye on you."

"Dear," Anna Lee said to her, "your mother is a woman of extreme character and integrity. I have truly enjoyed getting to know her during her stay in our community, and I can assure you that we're all here for one purpose, and one purpose only. To see that Mrs. Lassiter gets reelected."

"And who are you?" my daughter asked Anna Lee.

"Why, I'm one of your mother's dearest friends. My name is Anna Lee Benton, and I have more money than you'll ever accumulate in ten lifetimes of your own, so I will thank you to show a little more respect to your mother in front of me."

"Well, I'm sorry, Mrs. Benton," my daughter said, "but you don't know my mother as well as you think you do. She's an anarchist. When she told me about this event and her involvement in its planning, I was thrilled at first. Even took her shopping for a new outfit. I thought she had finally come to her senses and was going to be a normal person for once in her life. But then my husband met with the contractor rebuilding her house, and he found out about my mother's unusual floor-plan reconfiguration requests."

This wasn't going to go well for me.

"She's turning one of the bedrooms into a wet room. Tiled from floor to ceiling with shower jets coming out of the walls from every direction. She's turning another bedroom into some sort of den of iniquity. The contractor couldn't even find the words to describe the various functions of the apparatus my mother was having installed. But I know my mother. She's planning on having a party house where everyone with any kind of fetish is welcome to explore their fantasies to their fullest. When I found out about all this, I knew my mother hadn't changed one bit. And that's why I'm here tonight.

Whatever she's got cooking up in that brain of hers, I won't let her get away with it."

My daughter then stormed off to the bar to get a drink. Anna Lee was pretty shocked by her accusations against me, and frankly, so was I. She was way off base. That wet room was nothing more than a personal dream of mine. I'm a Pisces. I like water. What can I say? And that "den of iniquity," as my daughter put it, was going to be a legitimate massage room. I worked as a masseuse years ago and still had my license. I hadn't told anyone this, but I decided two months ago to give up my herbal supplement side gig permanently, which meant I was going to have to find a new source of income. It's hard for a girl to get by on little more than a social security check each month!

Okay, so my masseuse techniques are a bit unconventional, but they work. The thing about the herbal supplement business was that I was getting tired of thinking about the risk factor. I mean, sure, spending a few months or even a year in jail if you get caught when you're in your fifties wouldn't have been a pleasant experience, but getting caught when you're pushing seventy is a whole different matter. I needed a side hustle that wouldn't land me in jail someday.

Anyway, I explained the whole thing to Anna Lee, and she seemed to accept what I had to say. Whether she was simply being kind or if she truly believed me, I wasn't sure. But thankfully she dropped the subject. I asked her if she wanted me to bring her some appetizers from the buffet, but she said she was perfectly capable of getting them for herself, though she appreciated the gesture. As we both stood up together to head in that direction, another guest who had just entered the room caught my eye.

"Millie?" he mouthed as our eyes met, since he was still too far away for me to hear him.

Again, instant recognition. It was becoming a theme for the evening.

"Dean?" I said as I narrowed the gap. "Is that really you?"

"In the flesh!" he answered.

"I can't believe it. How long has it been?" I asked, even though I knew the answer.

"Too long. Far too long. Oh, the one that got away from me. Never thought I'd lay eyes on her again. But here you are. And look at you!" Dean said, and then continued in a whisper, "You're as beautiful now as you were all those years ago the last time I serviced you."

We both laughed. At least he knew where his talents lay. I asked him what he was doing here. He said he was the secretary of transportation, the token Republican member of our Democratic governor's cabinet. Figures. A car mechanic turned powerful politician, and a Republican to boot! If my count was accurate, that made three currently powerful Republicans that I had slept with four decades ago. Not bad!

25

Dean and I caught up on old times as we both headed toward the appetizer buffet, but our conversation was cut short when Lanie came up to us and tried to make the introductions. She wasn't too pleased when she realized we already knew each other, but I let it go. I knew she was used to being the queen bee in this particular social circle, and it unnerved her that she had some real competition in me. I couldn't fault her for that.

As soon as I had filled my plate, I made my excuses, left the two of them, and headed back toward the table. Rebecca had returned with her own plate, so we sat awhile and chatted. It didn't take long for me to pick up on her nervous energy, though. I asked her what was troubling her, and she said she wasn't sure she'd be able to last the night without opening her mouth and telling off some of the guests regarding their, as she put it, "ass-backward beliefs." I reminded her of our mission here, and for good measure, I told her that some of these guests probably thought the same about her own beliefs. She didn't like that one bit.

Gazing around the room, I thought most of the guests we had invited were probably already here. Looked like we were nearing capacity. But there were three people on the invite list whom I knew hadn't shown up yet. Bradley Williams, and Mr. and Mrs. Lassiter. I should have thought to get Bradley's cell number, but I hadn't, and I didn't know how to get in contact with him now to see why he was running late. He was our keynote speaker. He had to be here! And as far as the Lassiters went, well, I'd have to leave them to Lanie. But she was preoccupied at the moment, speaking with Speaker Shreves about something. I couldn't tell what, but she was very animated, her arms flailing about in every direction in excitement.

After several attempts, I finally made eye contact with her and gestured with my finger for her to make her way back over to the table.

"Lanie," I said as she took her seat, "have you noticed that we're missing a couple of very important guests?"

It took her a minute to scan the room, but that light bulb eventually turned on and her jaw practically dropped to the floor.

"She's not here," Lanie said.

"No, she's not. And neither is her husband. Nor Bradley Williams, for that matter. I don't have any way to get in contact with him, but do you have a way to reach the Lassiters?"

Without missing a beat, she retrieved her cell phone from her purse, thumbed through her contacts, and found the one for Mrs. Lassiter's campaign manager. A few moments later, we were reassured that the Lassiters were on their way and would be here momentarily. We both breathed a sigh of relief.

Bradley entered the room a moment later, and I went over to greet him, relieved that all the most important guests were now accounted for. I gave him a rundown of the agenda for the evening, letting him know that he'd be speaking after Chessy did her one-woman Sondheim review. So sometime after the main course was served.

"Bradley," I said, switching topics as I followed him over to the bar, "have you known the Lassiters long? I mean, I know she only recently switched parties and all, but don't politicians tend to cross aisles for social functions from time to time?"

"Rarely, these days. A shame, really. So, no, I don't know them personally, but now that she's a Republican, I'm sure I'll see her around. I have to say, Millie, that I'm still in a bit of shock over seeing you so engaged politically. When you and Lanie showed up at my office to ask me to come speak tonight, I was convinced my eyes and ears were deceiving me. Sure, people change, but I'm having trouble putting these two pictures together, the Millie I knew back in the day and the Millie standing before me now."

Damn, I thought. How was I going to convince him of what he already suspected was a lie? And even if I could, what was the point? He didn't know the Lassiters personally, so he wasn't going to be of much use in my quest to learn more about them.

I was just about to come clean to him, hoping that he wouldn't betray my confidences, when there was a bit of a commotion at the entrance to the room. Mr. and Mrs. Lassiter had arrived, and let me tell you, they were being treated like heroes as they entered. Bradley left my side and made his way over to introduce himself to them, so I returned to the table to find that both of my drinks from earlier had mysteriously disappeared.

"Where are my drinks?" I asked Rebecca, who was still sitting at the table.

"Julie. She's keeping a close eye on you and Chessy, and when I told her who the drinks belonged to, she confiscated them. She's got her faults, but she obviously cares about the people she looks after."

"That might be true, but I don't appreciate her treating me like I'm some sort of child who can't make decisions for herself."

"Fair enough, but as long as she's here with us tonight, you might as well abstain. She's not going to let you have any fun that she doesn't approve of."

Great. No alcohol, no marijuana, and I was starting to question our whole plan for the night. Why hadn't it occurred to me that the attendees weren't likely to have much in the way of intel on the Lassiters? Bradley didn't know them, and I doubted most of the other attendees did. It should have been obvious, since she only recently became a Republican. But I was still holding out hope that Speaker Shreves would be able to deliver. The problem was, I'd have a hard time getting him alone one on one to pump him for information. I was resigned to having Lanie do it, instead, and I was starting to wonder if she was forgetting the purpose of our presence tonight. She was having far too good a time schmoozing with her influential friends.

I decided to take matters into my own hands, though, and marched myself over to her, pulling her aside.

"Lanie," I began, "I'm afraid it's going to be up to you to carry on our mission. I just spoke with Bradley, and he said he didn't know anything about the Lassiters. I have a feeling we're going to get the same answer from most of the guests here. Sure, they're happy she's on their side now, but if Bradley's lack of experience with them is any indication, the others aren't going to be of much use either. That is, except for the speaker. If he's still the same guy I knew back in the day, he would have done his homework on her before agreeing to let her move to his side of the aisle. He's the one with all the power, right? Problem is, I got the sense from him that he's not interested in reminiscing with me over our shared past. Which means he's unlikely to acquiesce to my attempt at engaging him in conversation, period. You'll have to do it. Find out what he knows about them."

"I, uh, I'll try," she said. "It won't be easy."

"Try telling the speaker you want to make the Lassiters feel welcome in their new party, and it'd help if you could learn more about them. You know, so you can show them some true southern hospitality."

"That could work. You know they're not originally from here. They're from New York. Moved down here about ten years ago. Maybe a little longer."

"How did you find that out?"

"The speaker told me."

"See? You're already on the case! Now, go back over to him and be a good little detective."

She did as I instructed, but it turned out she needn't have bothered, because the next thing I knew, the proverbial shit hit the fan.

I heard a gut-wrenching wail and uncontrollable sobbing coming from the other side of the room. I spun around so fast that I nearly fell off my heels. But once I regained my balance, my eyes focused on a middle-aged man standing over Julie, who was sitting at a table with her face in her hands, weeping like there was no tomorrow. I rushed over as fast as I could, Lanie and the others hot on my trail.

"I don't know what I'm going to do!" Julie managed to say.

I asked the man standing above her what had happened, and all he could tell me was that he had asked her if she was married and whether she had any children. I sized up the situation pretty quickly. He was hitting on her and wanted to know if she was available. But anyway, the next thing he knew, she was sobbing and had no further explanation to give me. And it didn't take long for the entire room full of guests to converge upon our location.

"I loved him so much!" Julie continued as best she could. "And now I'm going to have to raise my baby without him. Alone. Single, with no support."

She rubbed her stomach, clueing everyone in on the fact that she was pregnant by a man she was no longer with.

"Julie," I said as I clasped her hand, "look around you. You're not alone. You have me and Anna Lee and Rebecca and Lanie and even Chessy. Your child is going to have five fairy grandmothers in its life. Your child will want for nothing. Anna Lee can support you both financially. Rebecca will make sure your child is well educated. I'll be the fun fairy grandmother. Chessy will teach your child about art and culture. And Lanie, well, we'll figure out her role later."

Yes, I know it was a bit brazen of me to presume that the other ladies would want to have any involvement whatsoever, especially given that some of them had grandchildren of their own. But I didn't know what else to say. I needed to calm her down, and the only way I could think of to accomplish that was to make sure she knew that she and her baby would have the support they needed.

"I miss him so much," Julie added as she began to recover. "I loved him more than I had ever loved another man. He was my soulmate. I didn't care that he also slept with men sometimes. He told me he was attracted to people, not genders. I didn't understand what that meant, but he said he loved me more than any other person he had slept with before."

Well, that answered one of the questions that had been simmering in my mind. Scott was indeed bisexual, and Julie knew. Not knowing what else to say, I looked up, and the crowd gathered around us. Lots of questioning faces stared back at me, some unsure of what to do next, some wanting more of an explanation, and others probably in shock at the mere mention of a bisexual man who loved people, not genders. So, I gathered my wits about me and came up with a plan to fill in some of the missing details for the rest of the guests. And I figured I'd kill two birds with one stone.

Speaking loudly enough for everyone to hear, but looking directly at Mr. and Mrs. Lassiter, I said, "Julie here was in a relationship with a wonderfully sweet, caring man. He was most recently employed at the Springtime Pastures community, teaching water aerobics classes for some of its residents, including myself. That's how the two of them met. She's the activities director for the part of the community I currently live in. A beautiful brick building with lovely, spacious residential units inside and a four-star dining establishment on the main level."

Rebecca, Lanie, Anna Lee, and Chessy all looked at me like I had no idea what I was talking about. Like how dare I give the food served in the B-Block dining room four stars. Which was a fair point, since we've all eaten there, though some more than others.

"Anyway," I continued, noticing the beginnings of a slight glimmer of recognition in Mr. Lassiter's eyes. "About a month ago, I got the surprise of my life when I showed up for my class with him, only to find him face down in the pool, dead."

There were gasps all around.

"But that's not all. He was a former Olympic athlete who had sustained an injury some years back, thereby ending his swimming career. He used to say the one thing he didn't miss about his former career was the Speedos he had to wear. He was very self-conscious about how he looked, not that he needed to be. He was an Adonis as far as I was concerned. You're probably asking yourselves why I'm mentioning this particular detail right now. The thing is, when I found him dead as a doornail, he was wearing a Speedo. And not the one I had given him for his birthday earlier, trying to coax him into giving us older ladies a bit of a show."

More gasps. I wasn't sure why, but I didn't care. I was on a roll. Mr. Lassiter began to squirm a little. Almost imperceptibly, but I noticed it and was betting others who were facing him did as well. I wasn't sure if he recognized me yet, but he certainly knew who I was talking about.

"At first, me and my companions here," I said as I pointed to the other ladies, "were in total shock. How could such a young, fit man just die like that? There were no obvious signs of foul play that we could see. No blood in the pool nor on the pool deck."

There was a collective sigh of relief, though I knew it would be short-lived.

"Well, we got to talking and decided to take matters into our own hands. With Julie's help, we did a little investigating. We searched his home. Nothing was out of place, at least not initially. But when we started going through his files and eventually his laptop, we began to realize that there were certain aspects of his life that we hadn't known about."

I had them eating out of my hands now.

"For example, we discovered that an anonymous benefactor, if you will, was transferring significant sums of money into his account on a monthly basis. We also found no evidence of any rent or mortgage payments for his house. We discovered a long trail of brokenhearted women whom he had either dumped or been dumped by after relationships that usually lasted only a couple of months."

There were puzzled looks all around now, except for Mr. and Mrs. Lassiter. *And* the speaker of the house, Michael Shreves.

"I think I've hit the highlights of our investigation. But what really surprised us, thanks to Cheshire Lively here," I said as I pointed to her, "was that the autopsy revealed that he died of a heart attack. A young man, still in the prime of his life, died of a heart attack. Furthermore, he died before he hit the water. For him to have ended up in the pool, either he had to have been standing right at the edge of the water when he died or someone relocated his body there from wherever he had the heart attack."

You could hear a pin drop, the room was that quiet, waiting for me to make my next move.

"What was his name?" Rebecca asked, egging me on.

"Scott Finch," I said, as I watched Mr. Lassiter begin to back away from the crowd.

He thought he was being subtle, but he wasn't, and everyone noticed.

"And that man," I said as I pointed directly at him, "knew Scott personally and for many years, according to the photos and videos we came across during the course of our investigation. When I confronted him a few weeks ago, he ran, just like he's attempting to do now."

26

"I have no idea who this woman is! I've never met her before!" Mr. Lassiter yelled over his shoulder as he turned his back on me to head toward the exit.

"Not so fast," I said as I motioned for Julie and Rebecca to head him off before he could escape.

They were the only other two of our group who were quick enough on their feet to intercept him. I was going to reel this fish in come hell or high water. He wasn't going to escape. Not this time. They reached him, each grabbing an arm and forcibly turning him back around to face me.

"You have nowhere to go, Mr. Lassiter. Nowhere to run, and no one else to hide behind. You have to stand on your own two feet right here, right now, and tell us what you know about Scott's death. And if you choose not to cooperate, we're going to turn all our evidence over to the state bureau of investigations. Everything we've got that links you to Scott. And I'm sure the SBI investigators will have no trouble finding out who that anonymous benefactor dumping large sums of money into Scott's account was. Though I could probably save them some time and simply give them your name, since I'm pretty sure it was you."

Mr. Lassiter stood there, dumbfounded, unable to speak. Meanwhile, out of the corner of my eye, I noticed Speaker Shreves taking Mrs. Lassiter aside, so I took a few steps in their direction, hoping to hear what he was going to say to her. And sure enough, I did. I've always been blessed with excellent hearing, catlike hearing as others have described.

"I thought I told you to take care of the situation," Speaker Shreves whispered to her. "But I didn't mean for you to kill him. Just make him go away."

So both she and the speaker knew. They knew her husband had some sort of relationship with Scott, and she was instructed by the speaker to make him disappear. I yanked her away from him and dragged her by her arm over to where her husband stood, still trapped by Rebecca and Julie but also now by Anna Lee, Chessy, and even Lanie.

"Go ahead, Mrs. Lassiter," I began, "enlighten us all on the arrangement you had with Speaker Shreves. You know, the one I overheard him reminding you of."

She didn't speak.

"Cat got your tongue? A shame. Well, here, let me help you," I said as I turned back toward the crowd. "Now I'm no investigative expert here, but I think I'm starting to put the pieces of this particular puzzle together. For reasons that are still unknown to me, Alicia Lassiter grew disaffected with her former party. She decided to switch. But before she could do it, she had to enter into some sort of arrangement with the speaker here. She wanted something, otherwise there would have been no real benefit for her. She still represents a pretty blue district, so running for reelection in her current district as a Republican wasn't going to work for her. She wanted something bigger in exchange for giving her new party a supermajority in the House. But before she could get it, the speaker had a condition of his own that she had to meet."

I was surprising even myself with the adeptness at which I was reasoning through all this on the fly. But I was sure I was on to something. I just wasn't sure what. What did she want? What did she want so badly that she was willing to go to such extraordinary lengths?

"Now I could speculate," I continued, "on what it was that she wanted. But I'd rather she tell us herself. So, Mrs. Lassiter, what did you want badly enough that you were willing to kill Scott to get it?"

"I didn't kill him," she responded.

"No, of course not. He died of a heart attack. I didn't say you actually killed him. But were you willing to?"

She clammed up.

"Did you know your husband was either having an affair or had had an affair with Scott?" I asked, running on a pretty strong hunch at this point. "Were you trying to, um, tidy up a loose end before announcing your party switch?"

Mr. Lassiter's head lowered ever so slightly but not so much in shame. More like simple acceptance that his secret had been revealed and that, quite possibly, his wife had already known.

"Why did Speaker Shreves instruct you to make Scott go away?" I then asked, eliciting a number of shocked expressions from most of the other guests. "I'm assuming you had to accomplish this before you could switch parties and get whatever it was that you were after. But why was it so important?"

Mrs. Lassiter refused to speak, but it seemed Mr. Lassiter could stay silent no longer.

"I wasn't having an extramarital affair with Scott," he announced.

"Then what would you call it?" I asked. "Because from where I'm sitting, it seems like you did. Why else would the speaker instruct your wife to make Scott go away?"

And then it hit me.

"Mrs. Lassiter," I said as I fixed my gaze on her, "were you the one having an affair with Scott? Our investigation only produced evidence of a connection between Scott and your husband, not between Scott and yourself. But now you have me wondering if, perhaps, Scott was a mutual friend with whom you were sleeping on the sly."

I felt a not so gentle tug on my sleeve and turned around to find my daughter's hand gently ripping the fabric of my dress, her nails puncturing holes too big to be repaired later.

"Mom," she whispered into my ear, "what the hell are you doing? The Lassiters are fine upstanding citizens, and you're acting like a crazy woman, accusing them of what, exactly? You have no proof that they had any involvement with the death of this Scott person. And you have no proof that either of them had an affair with him. You're embarrassing yourself, not to mention what you're doing to my reputation here."

"My child," I said, loudly enough for those closest to us to hear, "I'm proud of my crazy. It takes a crazy to know a crazy, and these Lassiter people are crazy. As is that speaker. But put a pin in him for a second. When this is all over, you and I are going to have a little chat about him and some of the other guests here. They're not who you think they are."

She yanked on my sleeve further, tearing it at the shoulder seam. Damn. I mean, it's not like I was ever going to wear this dress again, but the image of me accusing these people of attempted or planned murder with a ripped sleeve wasn't going to instill the confidence I wanted our guests to have in me. Well, to be fair, I had probably already blown my reputation with most of them anyway for having accused their new golden daughter of having an affair and possibly premeditating a murder. I wasn't sure, though, which they were more offended by. They'd probably have to take a poll of their constituents to figure that one out. Politicians, ugh.

Anyway, I tugged myself loose of my daughter and continued on.

"Mrs. Lassiter, I'm still waiting for your answer. Were you having an affair with Scott?"

"Your daughter was right," Mrs. Lassiter said after a brief pause. "You *are* a crazy woman. You should be locked up. You have no idea who you're dealing with here, and you are way out of your depth."

"She might be a little eccentric, but she's not certifiable," Lanie said, coming to my defense. "Millie here might be many things, but she's honest, and she's true."

"You're the one out of her depth here, Mrs. Lassiter," I added. "You're afraid, very afraid, and you should be. If you weren't having an affair with Scott, you would have said so. But you didn't. Instead, you have attacked me. Isn't that what politicians tend to do? When someone confronts them with an unflattering truth, all they do is attack their accuser instead of answering the charge. Well, you won't get away with that here. Not with me."

She didn't respond.

"Did your husband mention his little run-in with me at the library?"

Her eyes widened a bit, but only for a second before she recovered. One second too long, though. I had struck gold.

"Let me fill everyone in on this little rendezvous he and I had. I recognized him at the library. I went over to him and showed him a picture of Scott and mentioned that he had recently passed away unexpectedly. Mr. Lassiter ran without uttering a word. So, at the very least, he knew at that moment that Scott had passed, if not before then. But I'm betting he already knew. Almost like he was prepared for such a confrontation. Like someone was eventually going to ask him about Scott's death."

"I didn't kill him, and I had nothing to do with his death," Mr. Lassiter reiterated.

This time, I actually believed him. It was something about the way he said it, as if he wanted to make sure everyone knew that he hadn't, so that every witness here tonight would have no doubt of his innocence. I glanced at Chessy to see what she thought, and she nodded ever so slightly.

"I believe you now. I believe you didn't kill him and that you didn't have anything to do with his heart attack." I said to him. "In fact, I don't believe you were there at the pool the day he died at all. But you knew that he *had* died. Your wife told you, didn't she? Because she was there when it happened."

I really had no idea where these interrogation skills were coming from, but I was damn sure glad I was learning something new about myself! Mr. Lassiter looked like he wanted to say something further, but Mrs. Lassiter gave him a look that would have melted steel. I knew then, without a doubt, that she was the ringleader here. She was our culprit.

"Would you like to tell us, Mrs. Lassiter, how it happened?" I asked.

More silence from her, so I looked at him instead, pleading for any explanation or additional information he might be able to add. He was the weak link.

"Mr. Lassiter, you don't look like the type who would survive prison well. Even if you didn't have anything to do with Scott's death, you knew he had died. You knew how and when and that his body was left face down in a pool, making it look like he had simply drowned. I imagine a judge would look more favorably on you if you fess up to what you know now."

Mrs. Lassiter interrupted, stating that neither she nor her husband had anything further to say without the presence of their lawyer. And then she attempted to leave, but the other ladies blocked her way

"We had an arrangement with Scott," Mr. Lassiter said, much to the dismay of his wife.

"Oh?" I asked. "What kind of arrangement?"

"A, um, sort of a ménage à trois," he said.

More shocked gasps emanated from the other guests—well, except for the speaker.

"A what?" Lanie asked.

"A threesome," I said, barely recovering from my own shock. "It means, Lanie, that the three of them were romantically involved. At the same time. In the same room. Probably on the same bed."

Along Came Millie

This definitely wasn't on my list of anticipated revelations for the evening, but I decided to plow ahead.

"And how long had this ménage à trois arrangement been going on? Months? Years? Oh, now I see. The bank statements. The transfers. You had been keeping Scott up in that home, very nicely I might add, so that the three of you would always have a place to meet up for your group sex sessions."

Damn, I was on a roll.

"You even bought him that house, didn't you?" I continued.

I really should have looked up the deed to the property beforehand, but I was pretty sure I was right about this.

"Which means we're talking about a years' long arrangement now. Out of curiosity, did this arrangement start before or after you had your daughter? Not that I really need to know, but it'd be a helpful frame of reference to have. You know, in case I feel the urge to draw a timeline of events for the authorities. They'll want every pesky little detail, I am sure."

I was running on pure adrenaline now.

"Tell me, Mrs. Lassiter," I continued as a new line in this tangled web presented itself, "is your daughter, the one I met at the library that day, Scott's biological child?"

Why it hadn't occurred to me until now how much their daughter resembled Scott was beyond me. But better late than never! When I got no answer, I pressed on.

"Did Scott know? Did he know that he had fathered a child?"

"Yes," Mr. Lassiter replied. "He knew. I couldn't have children of my own, which he also knew. So when my wife became pregnant, we all knew."

"So your wife, before she could switch parties, had to make the biological father of the girl you raised as your own disappear."

No, that didn't make sense once I heard my words out loud. This kind of scandal would have rocked any politician, regardless of party affiliation. The only conclusion I could come up with was that it was something about her party switch. Something to do with Scott.

"Mrs. Lassiter," I said, testing out a theory, "you told Scott you were going to switch parties, didn't you? But it wasn't his mere existence that caused the speaker to instruct you to make him go away. I've never known, nor have I ever cared about Scott's political affiliation. But he cared about yours, didn't he?"

Mrs. Lassiter gave a very slight nod.

"And when you told him you were going to switch, he threatened you, didn't he? I mean, maybe not in a physical sense, but he threatened to expose your secrets if you went through with it. He threatened to tell the whole world about your ménage à trois and that your daughter was biologically his."

"Yes," she said, finally breaking her silence. "I couldn't let that happen. Not just for my sake but for my daughter's sake as well."

"So you went over to the pool at Springtime Pastures that morning to, what, plead with him? To try to convince him not to go through with the threat?"

"I called him and told him I wasn't going to switch. Told him I wanted to see him, and that I wanted to see him wearing my favorite Speedo of his. Wanted to have some fun with him in the pool before you ladies showed up for your class."

"But why the Speedo?" I asked.

"All I wanted was to see him in it one last time."

"And why didn't you bring your husband with you? Did you and Scott, umm, have relations on occasion without him?"

"We both did," she said. "Sometimes we couldn't find a sitter for our daughter, so we'd take turns going over to Scott's."

Mr. Lassiter nodded in agreement.

"So arranging to meet with Scott on your own didn't arouse any suspicions with him. But you obviously had a different plan. You were going to threaten him back. But with what? What could you have held over his head to make him bend to your will?"

"He cheated during his last Olympic competitions. Took performance enhancing drugs to win."

"You mean, like steroids?"

"I never asked for details, but he knew what to take that wouldn't show up on a drug screen."

"And you were going to tell the whole world about it."

"I wouldn't have done it. I loved Scott. I just wanted him to think that I could."

"So you threatened him, and then he collapsed?"

"Well, not quite. I had a gun in my purse. No bullets. I would never have shot him, but I held the gun to his chest. That's when he collapsed. It was instantaneous. He fell softly, though, and right by the edge of the pool."

"Then you panicked."

"I checked for a pulse. Nothing."

"So instead of calling the paramedics, you rolled his body into the pool, figuring it would look like an accidental drowning."

She nodded but couldn't bring herself to say the words.

"I still have a couple of questions, though, if you don't mind. First, what was it that you wanted in exchange for your party affiliation switch?"

"I guess it doesn't matter now," she said. "I was promised a congressional seat."

"What do you mean, exactly? It's not like someone could simply hand you such a seat on a silver platter."

"Redistricting," Lanie interjected. "They were going to redo the districts to give her a reasonable shot at winning a congressional seat as a Republican."

"Can they do that?" Julie asked.

"Why not?" Rebecca answered. "Political parties on both sides have been doing it for years."

"So, Mrs. Lassiter," I said. "Just to make sure I understand. You were told that if you switched parties, you'd get a safe district to run in."

She nodded.

"Why was this so important to you?" I asked.

And then it hit me. Money. As a rising star in her new political party, a lot of doors were going to open for her. Speaking engagements. National TV interviews. Seats on various boards, if she wanted them. And a surefire way for her and her family to recover from that embezzlement scandal her husband had been caught up in. When she didn't respond, I chose to let the matter go. I didn't need confirmation of what I already knew to be true.

"You don't have to answer that last question if you don't want to, Mrs. Lassiter, but I do have one final question. Why was Scott so adamantly opposed to your party switch?"

"I think I know why," Julie said, preempting Mrs. Lassiter.

But before she could continue with her explanation, the doors to the dining room were flung open, and in walked a very tardy guest.

"Hey, everyone! Sorry I'm late! Hope I didn't miss the party!" the man said.

I realized who the voice belonged to before I identified the face. It was Randy, the cute but slightly stupid video store-clerk from my past who kept trying to hit the play button even after my tape was already at its end for the evening. Well, he wasn't so cute anymore. His eyes met mine, and for the third time this evening, it was instant recognition.

Turned out he was the state superintendent, head of the Department of Public Instruction. I suppose all those years of experience working with videos paid off, now that so much of education is done virtually. Well, I was four for four. Four men who could have been my daughter's father. All four were here, and all four were influential Republicans of varying degrees.

It took some doing, but after I promised not to further interrogate the Lassiters, I managed to wrangle the four men together and brought them to where my daughter was sitting, trying to disassociate herself from me.

"For nearly forty years," I said to her, "you have wanted to know who your father was. Well, now's your chance to find out. Or at least narrow it down."

She looked at me, obviously not comprehending what I was saying. The men, however, began to shift uneasily; they realized what I was about to say.

"One of these four men is your biological father."

MESSAGE FROM THE AUTHOR

I hope that you have enjoyed this fun-filled novel. I encourage you to sign up for my email list to get up-to-date communications on future releases.

Joshua Berkov's Email List Signup Page:

https://mailchi.mp/333d8ebe2cc8/exclusive-content-sign-up-form

ALSO BY JOSHUA BERKOV

The Enlightenment Series Novels

The Enlightenment of Angeline

The Enlightenment of Esther

The Enlightenment of Iris

The Enlightenment Series Shorts

The Nasty Lady Librarian of Shelbington

Shelbington Sweets

Standalone Novel

Adulting at the Moto-Lodge

ACKNOWLEDGMENTS

First and foremost, I would like to thank Alison Imbriaco, my editor, for her excellent attention to detail and for ensuring that this book contains no glaring, embarrassing errors.

I would like to thank my friends Paul Ray Heinrich and Marlene Debo for proofreading the final manuscript and doing so on a quick timeline.

I would like to thank my godmother Ellen Bradley for reading the book, chapter by chapter, as I was writing it. She helped keep me going when I didn't know where to take the story next.

Finally, I would like to thank all of my fans who have encouraged me to keep writing. My first novel was also going to be my last. But all of the positive feedback I have received has given me the confidence to continue honing my craft in the hope that I can continue to spread much laughter and joy through my writing.

ABOUT THE AUTHOR

Joshua Berkov is a librarian by day and a writer by night. He holds an AB in Philosophy from Brown University, an MSLS from the University of North Carolina at Chapel Hill, and an MBA from East Carolina University. He lives with his partner and two cats in Raleigh, North Carolina, though he is originally from Los Angeles, California. Josh is an avid reader and enjoys exploring new authors and genres on a regular basis. Nothing gives him greater pleasure than to make those around him laugh out loud.

- facebook.com/Joshua-Berkov-112600270508248
- x.com/JoshBerkov
- instagram.com/joshuaberkov

Made in United States
Troutdale, OR
08/02/2024